LOVED CYBORG

BOUND BY HER SERIES - BOOK 2

NELLIE C. LIND

SENSE OF ROMANCE

$\mathscr{S}$ense of $\mathscr{R}$omance

High-level romance for romance lovers!

Loved Cyborg
Bound by Her - Book 2
Copyright © Nellie C. Lind 2017
Cover and layout: Nellie C. Lind
Editor: Chrissy Szarek
Publisher: Sense of Romance
First edition
ISBN: 978-91-983127-7-5

ABOUT THE AUTHOR

Nellie C. Lind lives in Sweden with her son, but she was born in Poland. Writing has always been one of her greatest interests. Today, she runs the publishing house, Sense of Romance.

She writes passionate paranormal romance, fantasy, and science fiction books for adult readers. You'll find all sorts of beings in her stories, such as angels, vampires, gods, and elves.

You'll also find everything from short stories to novels among her books. Keep an eye open for upcoming releases!

Website: www.nellieclind.com
Facebook: www.facebook.com/nellieclind
Instagram: www.instagram.com/nellieclind

PROLOG

"Please, don't make me do this." Wind looked into Diane's beautiful blue eyes from where he stood by the window in the living room.

She sat on the bright sofa with a white blanket over her legs. Her skin was paler than usual, she'd lost a lot of weight over the past few months, and her hair lacked vitality. Her cheeks were flushed from the fever that tormented her body, and there was nothing he could do to help her.

He was losing her.

"It's either Celise or a woman MedAct will introduce you to, Wind. The doctors can't cure my leukemia. Besides, I can't hide how sick I really am anymore from everyone. Phoebe and Shade have already figured out I don't have minor heart disease."

"I know." His chest tightened. Sorrow filled him. He

didn't want to talk about this, but the conversation was inevitable. Who knew how long Diane had left? Judging by her appearance, it wasn't long.

"I don't want to force you. The final decision must be yours."

"If I don't do it, I'll die with you."

"Or end up with the Fighters."

Wind clenched his fists. *That* was the last thing he wanted. He remembered Silver and the other Fighters when Nightmare had imprisoned him, Shade, Phoebe, and Faye in the abandoned house. The crazed looks in their eyes, the aggression, and the madness that had lingered in their minds was enough for him to never want anything to do with them again. "Why her?"

"Because she loves you."

He took a deep breath and looked through the window when he heard a noise.

Celise's car turned into their driveway. She was as usual on time.

Wind recalled the day when he'd opened his eyes and seen Diane for the first time. She'd smiled, and the love in her eyes had filled him with joy. She'd been so beautiful.

His time as a newborn cyborg had been amazing. He'd been overprotective of her but hadn't had any issues adapting, and once they'd left MedAct, they'd been happy together for fifteen years.

Now, those fifteen years were coming to an end.

"She's so different."

"She is, but she's also a doctor, and she works for MedAct. She'll be able to take care of you once I'm gone."

He hated this. "But she's nothing like you. She might be a doctor, but you're an artist, like me. Your paintings are on a level few can reach, and that's why you were able to make enough money to create me. You gave me my artistic skills. They are what makes me ... *me*. How am I ever going to be happy with someone who's so different?"

Diane didn't answer. She didn't have an answer. "Do you at least *like* her?"

Wind hesitated. "She's a friend, so yes, I like her."

A gentle smile curved her lips. "That's a start, and besides, you won't have to move far. She lives here in Glaswell as well, taking care of all the cyborgs."

Everything within him protested. He didn't want this. He wanted to stay with Diane until the very end. He wanted to die with her, but that wasn't what she wished. "Would it make you happy if I bonded with her?"

Diane nodded.

He turned his gaze back to Celise, who'd gotten out of her car. The agony in his heart only grew as he swallowed and tried to control his rapid breathing. "Then I'll ask her."

CHAPTER 1

Celise shut the car door.

With a deep breath, she stepped in front of the two-story villa that belonged to Wind and Diane. It was a decorated masterpiece in light blue colors and a black roof. The colorful flowers and the white curtains reminded her of a castle. Diane and Wind had spent a lot of time creating the perfect home for them.

Wind.

Her heart clenched.

He and Diane fit perfectly together. It was obvious every time she saw them. She and Wind, on the other hand, were too different. She was the doctor and the scientist. He was the painter and the artist.

After her medical education at MedAct, Celise had started taking care of all the cyborgs in Glaswell, including Wind. She came by from time to time to make sure everything was all right, and today was such a day. She hated and loved these days because she *loved* him. She had for many years and being near him was difficult. The desire to touch him often became too much to handle.

Nerves swept over her as she approached the door. She knocked and tried to calm down, but her heart pounded, unwilling to relax. Even if she'd been here many times before, she always had the same reaction, always had a hard time being herself in front of him.

Someone approached the door.

Celise tensed even more, and when Wind opened it, blood rushed to her face. She could do nothing but stare at his handsome features. They pulled her in like a flower to the sun. He gave her that gentle smile she loved so much, with his plump and wide lips, and the caring gaze in his mesmerizing aluminum-colored eyes made her insides melt. The glow in them didn't ease the powerful impression he'd always had on her.

His light-brown hair hung over his broad shoulders. He was dressed in simple black sweatpants and a black t-shirt. Paint stains decorated both garments, and there was even a green dot on his cheek.

The soft scent of paint came off of him, and Celise couldn't help but smile. "Um ... hi ... That's a nice ... shirt." She cringed on the inside. Could she have said something more stupid?

Wind's lips twitched. "You like dirty shirts, Celise?"

She shrugged. It'd be best if she just remained silent before more foolish things came out her mouth, but when she noticed the sadness in his gaze, she couldn't help but take a step closer. "Are you all right?"

He nodded. "I'm fine. Come inside." He moved from the door and allowed her to enter.

It was like stepping into a fairytale in light blue and white. The wide and well-lit hallway was filled with amazing landscape paintings, two pillars, and a huge chandelier. In front of her was a white staircase with a beige carpet attached to every step.

Celise followed Wind to the second floor.

The smell of more paint hit her nose as she entered his study. It was a big and bright room with huge windows. There were brushes, cans with dirty water, and canvases all over the place.

She'd been there many times before and never grew tired of the beautiful paintings on the walls and the floor. It was like looking at landscapes of mountains and forests that looked so real she almost believed they were.

Celise approached his couch and the table that stood near it. "Why am I here so soon, Wind? I examined you just two weeks ago." She didn't mind being here again for a basic examination, not at all. An examination meant she could touch him without it being *wrong*.

"Diane wanted you to check me again."

"Did I miss something last time?"

There was that sadness in his eyes again. "Let's find out."

Diane wanted her to examine Wind for no apparent reason? That sounded strange, but if that was what she wanted, then Celise would do it. "All right." She put her bag on the couch.

She opened it and took out a small box, but before she got the chance to do more, Wind stepped in front of her. He invaded her personal space, and the deep gaze he gave her sent shivers down her spine. "Why are you—?"

"Do you like me, Celise?" he asked. "Do you like what you see when you look at me? Is it all right for me to stand this close to you?"

Celise almost jumped out of her skin.

What was this? Some kind of interrogation?

Something was up, but she couldn't pull herself together to ask what. His nearness affected her in ways it'd never done before. He'd never looked at her the way he did now. He'd never stood this near before either.

Silence lingered between them.

Wind never looked away, he never said anything, but his eyes whispered of emotions she was unable to read. The sorrow in them spoke of a secret she wanted to know. It was mixed with a pinch of curiosity, and when his gaze

13

traveled down her body, she couldn't help but tense.

Without warning, he grabbed the bottom of his shirt and took it off.

Celise gasped. "Oh, shit."

Warmth gathered between her legs as she stared at his fit and muscular body. Solid muscles and a six-pack filled her hungry gaze.

She swallowed. Would never get used to this. She'd examined him many times over the years, but seeing him without a shirt only got her going in the worst kind of way. The need to touch him, to gently glide her hand down his chest was difficult to hold back.

"Is something wrong?" Wind asked.

Celise snapped out of the spellbinding effect he had on her and turned to her bag. She searched through it frantically. "Where's that damn scanner?"

"You're holding it."

She froze and looked to her other hand, and true, she was holding it.

Damn, that was embarrassing.

Her cheeks were on fire, and she couldn't stop herself from looking at him again. His wide shoulders, slim waist, defined biceps, and large hands got her fantasy going.

She wanted him so badly. If she just could ...

"You didn't answer my question, Celise."

She winced. "What?"

Wind moved even closer, too damn close. All she'd have to do was tilt her head a little bit, and she'd have his lips against hers.

He caressed her arm. The touch made her tremble. "Do you like me, Celise?" His voice was like a seductive whisper that sent goosebumps all over her body, igniting that undying fire within her, making it more and more difficult to breathe.

"You know I do." Celise was unable to keep her voice steady.

"Yes, I know."

She studied his kissable lips, and couldn't hold back anymore. Her self-control was gone. He was too close, too tempting, too appealing. Her body acted on its own as she leaned closer and pressed her lips to his.

Heat and softness hit her. She closed her eyes and opened her mouth to deepen the kiss, but before she was able to make another move, Wind jerked away.

Celise opened her eyes and stared where he stood about five feet away. His eyes were wide, his massive chest heaved as he tried to catch his breath, and an underlying anger radiated from him.

Perfect.

She'd screwed up.

Big time.

Shame and pain flooded her. Celise considered

apologizing, but then it hit her. It might not have been his intention, but *he'd* caused this. Him being close was too much for her to handle. He knew that. She had so much desire burning within her that one gentle push was all it took for her to lose her mind. "Why'd you do that?" She kept her voice low.

"I ... I ..." He looked shocked, but the anger wasn't there anymore, thankfully.

"You should put your shirt on." She put the scanner in her bag. "I have no idea why Diane wanted me to examine you, but I can't do it. Not now." She zipped the bag and threw the strap over her shoulder. "I should go ..." She made for the door.

Wind grabbed her arm. "I'm sorry, Celise."

His anger might be gone, but *hers* was awakening. She was tired of this. Tired of always wanting him. He was always on her mind, always in her daily fantasies. Celise couldn't make it stop. Her heart just refused to let him go, and after all these years, it would never happen.

She had to make a drastic decision. It was either stay local and keep tormenting herself, or move to a place far away. Never see him again. That tore her open on the inside, but it was the only way. If she stayed, she'd live a half-life, always longing for someone she could never have.

Celise jerked her arm from his grip. "Don't touch me."

16

She wasn't the angry type, but he'd pushed her too far. His touch made everything inside her boil over. "Why did you do that?" she demanded again with an irritated voice, and she tensed her jaw. She glared at Wind. "Did you expect me to react differently? You know how much I want you, and we both know you'll never be mine, and yet, you behaved as if you were trying to seduce me." She took a few breaths. "Maybe there *is* something wrong with you, but I'm not staying around to find out what."

She started for the door again, only to find Diane standing there. It had been two weeks since she'd seen her, and her friend looked weaker than ever.

Diane had to use a cane to support herself. Her once beautiful eyes looked hollow, and her skin was pale.

Wind went to her as he put his shirt back on. "You shouldn't be up, my love."

Hearing Wind calling Diane "*my love*" hurt Celise more than usual.

Diane gave him a gentle smile. "I heard Celise yelling at you. I figured I should come and explain."

Confusion struck her. "Explain what?"

Wind helped his bound one to the couch.

"I'm sorry, Celise. It's my fault Wind came close to you."

Celise's gaze narrowed. "What do you mean?"

She watched Wind sit at Diane's side. He took her hand in his, and the love in his eyes made Celise want to turn

17

around and walk away again.

"Please, sit down, Celise." Diane pointed at the armchair in front of the couch. "I'll explain everything."

CHAPTER 2

"Why would you ask such a thing of Wind?" Celise asked as she sat and placed her bag next to her on the floor.

Diane smiled but wasn't able to hide the grief in her eyes. "I'm dying."

She winced, not expecting her to say that. "Yes, I know." She took a deep breath. "It's not Heart Disease you have, is it?" Her voice was low, filled with sadness.

"No, it's not, and I'm sorry I lied about that. I have leukemia."

Disbelief filled Celise. "Why would you make all of us believe you had heart disease?"

"So you wouldn't worry, but Phoebe and Shade already figured it out some time ago, and I guess you did, too."

"I'm a doctor. Your symptoms didn't match with the ailment you claimed to have."

Diane was one of her best friends. They'd known each

19

other for over five years, ever since Celise had moved to Glaswell to take care of the cyborgs. They'd always gotten along, and it didn't matter that Diane was ten years older. Seeing her like this was difficult.

"If I'm lucky, I have a few months left to live," Diane said. "As you can see, I can barely walk anymore because of the pain. I have no appetite, and I just want to sleep all the time." She closed her eyes for a second. She looked so tired.

Celise clenched her jaws. "You should've told me sooner. I could've helped you around the house, make life easier for you."

Her friend smiled gratefully. "Thank you, but Wind helps me out."

"Oh." She licked her lips. "Is there anything else I can do?"

"Yes, I need your help with something. I invited you here today to talk about it."

Celise nodded. "Anything."

Diane looked at Wind with an unspoken question in her eyes.

He gave her a sad smile and hugged her hand before he nodded.

Something was definitely going on.

"Aren't you curious about why I called you to examine Wind so soon?"

Celise frowned. "I thought at first something had happened to him, but when he opened the door and looked fine—"

"And then he touched you."

Celise avoided Diane's gaze. "He did." She couldn't get away from the feeling that she'd betrayed her friend. She wasn't supposed to touch Diane's cyborg, and yet, she had.

The last thing Celise wanted was a conflict. That was why she'd never mentioned her feelings for Wind, but he'd figured it out a few years ago. It was obvious Diane knew too.

Diane turned her gaze to Wind. "Did you like being close to Celise?"

"Yes, I did, but I wasn't prepared for the kiss."

Celise stared at them with a pounding heart.

"The kiss couldn't have been bad," Diane said.

"No, it wasn't. I registered her lips as soft and warm. She wanted more, but I moved away. My bond wasn't happy with me touching her." He sighed. "I'm sorry, Diane. I didn't see it coming. I shouldn't have moved away. I should've let her kiss me, but she has never touched me like that before." He gave Celise a gentle smile. "She's been a true friend, despite her feelings for me."

She sucked in air. Couldn't believe Wind had just said all that.

"If she kissed you again, would you accept it?" Diane asked.

Wind thought for a while. "Maybe, if my bond didn't object."

"It objects because you're bound to me. The bond makes you uninterested in any other woman."

"True."

Celise flew up from the armchair. Her body trembled, her vision went fuzzy for a short moment. "What the heck are you two talking about?"

"Please, sit down," Diane said. "I invited you here to examine Wind, but in fact, I wanted him to see if he'd find you appealing."

"And I do," Wind said. "You don't awaken any repulsive feelings within me, and why should you? We've been friends for many years."

Upsetting emotions pounded in her body like mad fires. Wind's words didn't make her feel any better. He made his so-called interest for her sound so clinical, so cold. "Why? What are you two trying to do? Break my heart?"

"No. Celise, don't you understand? You're the intelligent one here," Diane said.

She snorted. "My mind's toast right now, so please spell it out, because it feels like you two are conspiring something behind my back." She looked at Diane. "You're his bound one, and you're allowing him to touch another woman. You're even encouraging him to ... to see if he'll like it. Who does a thing like that? I mean what—?"

Then it hit her.

"Oh, my God." Her legs gave out, and her bottom hit the chair hard. Her emotions spun into havoc, unable to grasp, but it made sense now. The early visit, Wind's nearness, Diane's and his weird conversation.

Diane wanted her to take over Wind's bond.

"I don't want him to suffer, Celise, but the choices are few. It's either a woman MedAct will introduce him to or *you*. If you don't take over the bond, he risks death or joining the Fighters. I don't want either of those for him. I want him to live, to be happy."

Celise wiped away a tear running down her cheek. "Why me?"

"Because you're the best option. You already know Wind, and you love him."

She barely dared to look at him but forced herself to do so. "You agreed to this?"

"Yes. What else was I supposed to do?" Wind smiled, but his words hurt like hell.

He had *no* interest in her. His affection for her was from years of friendship. He didn't see a potential partner in her.

"I know what you're thinking," Diane said. "And you know it's the bond that makes him incapable of loving another woman the way he loves me, but once the bond is transferred to you, his love will be yours. You'll be able to have the relationship you've always wanted with him."

Celise didn't answer. She clenched her fists instead. She didn't like the way Diane talked about Wind and the bond. She knew how it worked, of course, but now when she was faced with it; it was a completely different story.

"You don't mind this?" She gave Diane a pained gaze.

Diane smiled faintly. "No, not when it's you. You've always been an amazing friend, despite your feelings for Wind, and I want what's best for the both of you."

Celise could only nod.

Shade, Phoebe, Wind, and Faye had told her what had happened in the wastelands when Nightmare had kidnapped Phoebe.

The Fighters believed the bond wasn't real, that they could exist without it. Nightmare had even tried to cut Shade from his bond but had failed. The rogue leader believed he was setting Shade free.

"This all sounds so ... fake," she said. "Maybe the Fighters were right."

"The bond is real to me, Celise." Wind's gaze was serious. "I don't agree with the Fighters' beliefs. The bond is part of my programming, and it makes me feel all these amazing things for Diane. It's what makes me ... *me*. Do you understand? I want her, and I'll want you once the bond is yours."

24

She frowned. "And what do *you* want now?"

"I want Diane to live. It's tearing me apart to watch her fade away. The doctors do everything they can, but the healing isn't working."

"So ... you're doing this for Diane. You don't *really* want me. You have no interest in me whatsoever." Celise needed him to say it.

Silence filled the room.

He remained still, just watched her with an unsure expression.

"Say it," she demanded.

Wind opened his mouth, but nothing came out.

She stood and approached him. "Say it. I need to hear you say what you really want. Do you have the slightest interest in me? Are you interested in more than friendship between us?" Her body trembled. Tears pressed behind her eyes, threatening to push forward any second.

This wasn't just the longest day in her life; it was the worst day in her life.

Wind took a deep breath. "No."

CHAPTER 3

"Thank you," Celise said. "That was all I needed to hear."

Wind watched her return to the armchair and pick up the bag before throwing it over her shoulder. With fast and upset steps, she headed for the door.

He gazed at Diane. His hands began to tremble as fear filled him. It looked like he wouldn't have a relationship with Celise after all. She'd left the room and was leaving, taking his chance for survival with her.

Diane nodded, telling him with unspoken words to go after Celise.

Wind ran after her.

She was almost at her car when he reached her.

"Please, Celise. Wait."

She ignored him and opened the car door. She threw her bag on the passenger seat.

He grabbed her arm just before she managed to get

inside. With a few swift moves, he closed the door, whirled her around to face him, and pushed her against the car, locking her between his arms. Adrenaline pumped in his body, making him breathe heavily.

Wind's heart clenched from the hurt in her eyes. It was all his doing, but it hadn't been his intention. He didn't want to hurt Celise. She was dear to him, but he didn't want to lie to her either. He didn't love her. He couldn't love her. He was bound to Diane. It was impossible for him to feel anything for her but friendship.

But, he needed her. Wind was afraid of what would happen once Diane died, and it was bound to happen, soon. He didn't want to be taken to MedAct to be bound to a stranger, and he didn't want to become one of the Fighters. He somehow had to convince Celise that *she* was his best option.

The thought of becoming hers made him shudder, but he pushed the feeling aside. It was just his bond objecting. It told him Diane was his bound one and he should stay with her. That he, under no circumstances, should deepen his relationship with Celise.

"Please listen to me," he said. "I understand how you feel. Believe me, I do, but give me a chance. Let me prove to you I can do this."

Celise snorted. "You're not doing this because you care about me or because you want to be with me. You're doing this to save yourself."

Wind held his breath. She was right, and that hurt. "Then help me get past this."

They looked at each other in silence.

He placed his hand on her arm. The warmth of her skin grazed his palm.

Wind tried to imagine what it'd be like to touch her, to caress her the way he'd caressed Diane so many times. He imagined Celise naked in his bed with passion in her eyes. Saw himself leaning over her, his hands exploring her body, but as soon as the image entered his mind, his bond went crazy.

His stomach twisted, nausea washed over him. Wind groaned and backed away. For a split second, he almost threw up.

Surprise filled him. He'd never expected the bond to react like that from a simple thought. He'd never thought of another woman in an intimate way before. Never been interested, never needed to, but realization swept over him. To become Celise's would be more difficult than he'd ever anticipated.

He'd deal with it. Had no choice.

But first, he had to convince her.

Thankfully, the nausea lasted only for a short while. Wind exhaled and straightened as the agony faded. He raised his gaze and looked right in the eyes of a worried Celise.

She seemed just as surprised by his reaction as he was.

"What just happened?" she asked with wide eyes.

Wind cleared his throat. "I ... um ... thought about you, and my bond didn't like it."

Celise blinked, her eyes going slightly wider. "You mean, you imagined us—" A blush decorated her sweet cheeks.

His lips twitched. He liked that color on her. "Yes, I did. It was just a simple thought of you naked in my arms, and my bond instantly protested."

She remained quiet for a few seconds, studying him. "I've never seen a cyborg react like this before."

"That's probably because cyborgs never imagine other women in their arms. The few times I've kissed you on the cheek was never an intimate act." He took a deep breath.

She crossed her arms. "So how exactly are you expecting this to work?"

Wind tensed. "I don't know."

Celise sighed and lowered her head. "I love you too much to let you die, you know that, don't you?"

He nodded, not sure where she was going with this.

"But you're choosing me for the wrong reason, Wind. What if MedAct can find you a better bound one? Hasn't that thought crossed your mind? We're nothing alike. I'm nothing like Diane." She shut her eyes. "Would you even be happy with me?" Her voice was barely a whisper.

She looked like she needed a hug, but she also needed someone who listened and understood. She needed *him* to be that person, but he couldn't.

Just the thought of Diane in his arms made his body respond. He'd always been there for her and she'd always been there for him. He doubted he'd ever have anything like that with Celise. With her, he expected complications, and yet, he was willing to give it a chance. "Don't give up on me. I might not have answers now, and I have no idea how to proceed, but I want to try. I want to try with you."

She scowled. "To live, not to *be* with me."

Frustration awakened within him. "I can't help what I feel. You know how the bond works. You're asking for the impossible right now, but believe me when I say I care about you. You're my friend, and yes, we're different, but we've always been able to get along. If you just give us time, I believe we can make this work." He couldn't believe he was saying all that when just minutes before she'd arrived, he'd assumed the opposite.

Celise finally looked at him but didn't say anything.

"Jade Silva is coming by tomorrow. I hope she'll be able to give us some answers. I'd like you to be there."

She winced. "Why?"

Wind swallowed. "Because before she leaves, I must tell her how I wish to proceed. My bond must be transferred to someone else before Diane dies. I was hoping to tell Jade you wish to take Diane's place, but if you won't, we will go to MedAct, and stay there until the bond is transferred to ... someone." The thought made him shiver.

Silence lingered between them once more.

He watched her, waiting for her answer. He'd never paid much attention to Celise's looks before, but he did now even if his bond protested. At least, it wasn't painful this time, just uncomfortable.

Her light blonde hair was put into a ponytail. Only a few strands hung free, and he *liked* looking at her sweet and doll-like appearance. Her heart-shaped face and green eyes made him see the innocence she radiated.

If she wanted, she could create a cyborg of her own. She'd passed MedAct's tests without a fuss, but she'd never applied. Her love for him stood in the way, and Wind suspected she'd only try to create a cyborg just like him, and that wasn't what she wanted. She wanted *him*, not a copy of him. Besides, it wouldn't be fair to the newborn cyborg.

"So what do you say, Celise? Will you come by tomorrow at noon?"

She remained silent, and the doubt in her eyes made him tense. For a few short seconds, he held his breath, just waiting for her to say something - anything.

The underlying sadness in her expression showed him the truth.

He was going to lose her too.

"I love you so much it hurts," Celise finally said, "but I can't bind you to me and spend the rest of my life knowing you chose me to save yourself, or because you didn't want to be with a stranger. If you want me to show up tomorrow, I need *you* to give me something to go on. And I need it now."

Wind stood stunned. She might as well have asked him to bring down the moon. His mind was blank, but his body acted on its own. His heart pounded when he placed his palms on her cheeks. Her skin was smooth and warm, but the intimate touch made his bond protest anew. It didn't like what he was planning, but he had to do it. Had to make Celise understand he *could* see beyond the bond.

When she'd kissed him in his study, he hadn't been prepared, but he was prepared now.

He swallowed and took a step closer. Nausea hit him again and his head begun to spin, but he tried to ignore it.

Celise didn't move. She just kept watching him. Waiting … but her hands trembled.

Wind said a silent prayer, hoping his bond would understand. He leaned closer and picked up a gentle scent of vanilla coming from her. It made him smile. Diane used vanilla perfume too sometimes.

He tilted his head, slowly moving into place. Then he pressed his lips against hers.

Celise gasped.

Just like last time, her lips were soft and warm, but this time he noticed she had a tasteless balm on. It didn't bother him because Diane used that as well. Wind wrapped his arms around her and pressed her closer to his chest.

His breath mingled with hers as he opened her mouth with his, deepening the kiss, but ignoring the growing agony wasn't easy. His stubbornness kept him from pulling away, despite his bond screaming for him to let go.

She moaned and wrapped her arms around him. Celise responded to his kiss in a way he hadn't expected. At first, she was stiff, unsure, but it didn't take long before her hands ended up on his body, caressing him, stroking his hair. It was a passionate whisper of her hunger for him, of the love she'd pushed aside for so many years. It was all coming to the surface, and the further she went, the fiercer the agony became.

When she grabbed the top of his sweatpants, his bond attacked him.

Wind jerked away and let out a scream as his head was filled with sharp agony from every direction. The nausea he'd felt before was nothing compare to now. He doubled over, almost unable to remain standing, but somehow, managed not to fall.

Slowly, the pain subsided.

After almost a minute, he was able to straighten his

back and exhale. He felt bruised, exhausted. This wasn't something he wanted to experience again anytime soon, but something told him it would happen sooner than later.

He met Celise's glazed eyes. Her cheeks were flushed, and passion was written all over her face, but there was guilt as well. She bit her lip and clenched her fists, avoiding his gaze.

"I'm sorry," she said.

Wind took a deep breath, relaxing. "Don't worry about it."

She shook her head and grimaced. "I should've never asked this of you."

"You had every right."

"Are you all right?"

"No, but I'll be soon. My bond didn't like me touching you."

Celise nodded. "I figured, but I'm grateful you did. I don't know how we're ever going to do this if kissing me gives you such discomfort."

Hope awakened within him. "You mean you're willing to do this?"

"I'm willing to think about it. You gave me what I asked for, even if it hurt you. That says a lot." She got into her car.

There was nothing more Wind could do to keep her there, but the smile she gave him before she closed the door and drove away kept his optimism alive.

CHAPTER 4

Leaving Wind after their turbulent discussion was difficult. She'd wanted to turn back at least a thousand times during her five-minute drive home.

Celise wanted to tell him she'd be his bound one, that he couldn't have made her happier by asking her, but the thought of Diane tightened her chest.

For her dreams to come true, there had to be pain.

A lot of it.

She parked in her driveway. Her single-story villa looked like a lot of other houses in the area. It was about fifteen hundred square feet, painted white, and with a black roof. A small lawn was in the front and no fence.

She lived on the south side of Glaswell where there were plenty of open spaces, beautiful homes, and parks. The shopping mall was just a few minutes away, and she loved spending time there.

The town was a calm and peaceful place. The clear blue sky, the warm summer weather, and the clean streets made her feel like she lived in paradise. She'd considered herself lucky, living in a place like this. Glaswell was also kept behind guarded walls, keeping unwanted visitors out.

Celise took a deep breath. She didn't feel like going inside. She needed to go for a walk ... to think ... to breathe.

She walked down the sidewalk slowly.

Her life had taken an unexpected turn. She didn't know much about how to transfer a bond. She'd always avoided studying that subject because of Wind. Now, she regretted that, but Jade knew and could teach her.

"You look like you have a lot on your mind."

She jerked when she heard the voice. "Faye?" She'd been walking for several minutes, not aware of where she'd been heading and had ended up in front of Faye's house. It looked similar to hers; white with a black roof.

Faye sat on a blanket on her lawn. She was dressed in simple sweatpants and a sleeveless T-shirt. Her blonde hair hung down one of her shoulders, and she held a book in her hands.

Shade and Phoebe lived across the street. They'd been home for a few days now since the incident with Nightmare and his Fighters. Their bond was restored, and they seemed happy.

Faye, on the other hand, was not her cheerful self

anymore. Not since she'd kissed Silver to save Shade from the Fighters. Where he was now, Celise didn't know, but she knew one thing. It wasn't over for Faye, far from it.

"Why don't you sit down and bother me a little? You look like you need it," Faye said with a wry smile.

She snorted. Faye may not be the same any longer, but she sure hadn't lost her attitude. Her suggestion was tempting though. Celise needed someone to talk to, and it seemed like Faye needed someone to talk to as well. She removed her shoes and took a seat.

Faye put her book down. "So what's eating you?"

Celise sighed. "Diane and Wind invited me over today. Diane wanted me to examine Wind, even though I did so just two weeks ago."

She raised an eyebrow. "Is that too soon?"

"Yes. I worried that something had happened to him, but he was fine."

"So why did they invite you over?"

Celise breathed deeply while she gathered her words. "Diane is dying." She didn't say anything else, letting Faye take in the news.

Her friend's smile faded, and her blue eyes widened. She stilled, and disbelief colored her face. "Oh, my God." Her voice trembled. "She told you that?"

"Yes, but I figured it out some time ago. Phoebe and Shade have figured it out as well."

Faye winced. "Am I the only one who doesn't know?"

"Diane didn't tell anyone, but since she told me now, I doubt it's a secret anymore."

"But why? Why keep such a thing secret?" She crossed her arms over her chest and anger radiated from her. "She and I sure are going to have a long talk." She shook her head. "Unbelievable. And they invited you over to tell you that?"

Celise shook her head. "No. You know what'll happen to Wind if Diane dies, don't you?"

Faye licked her lips. "He'll die, or become one of the Fighters if he by some miracle survives."

She nodded. "Exactly."

Her friend's eyes widened with new surprise, then a big grin spread on her lips. Excitement shone right through her, and a gentle laughter broke from her mouth.

It was amazing how fast she could switch from one mood to another.

"Oh, my God, Celise! You're going to be Wind's new bound one, aren't you? You've never spoken about it, but I've seen your interest for him. You must be thrilled!"

She tried to smile, but it came out stiff.

Faye frowned. "But you don't look thrilled. Aren't you happy? Don't you want to be with Wind?"

She slumped her shoulders. "I do. I really do, but he only wants me to save himself. He has no interest in me whatsoever. All I am to him is a way to escape death. I can't bind him to me because of that. It feels wrong, even if I love him." Celise sighed. "Tomorrow, Jade is paying them a visit, and Wind wants me to be there. If I don't come, he and Diane will go to MedAct to find someone else who wants to take over the bond."

Faye didn't move. She stared at her. "Well, that sucks."

Celise couldn't help but smile when Faye pouted. "You're not taking this seriously. I have no idea what to do."

"Of course you do! You become Wind's new bound one, no matter what he feels right now."

She blinked. "Just like that?"

"Yes, just like that." Faye put her hand on Celise's shoulder. "Hon, I love you, but you're looking way too much into this. He doesn't feel anything for you because of the bond, right?"

Celise nodded. "Right."

"Then from here on, you've two ways to go. You either become Wind's new bound one, or you don't. It's that simple, but trust me, you'll be happier with him than without him."

She looked at her hands. "If he's bound to another, I'll regret it for the rest of my life."

"Exactly, and is that what you want?"

Celise shook her head. "No."

"Then, you go there tomorrow, and tell them you'll take over the bond."

Faye's straight-forward way made her feel better, and she was right.

She was reading too much into this. Overthinking. Wind didn't love her *now* because he couldn't. It was unfair of her to demand more of him at this moment. "How about you?" Celise asked.

Faye pulled back. "What about me?"

"Have you heard anything about Silver?"

Her expression tensed. "No, nothing. It's been days since we were at the house, but to me, it feels like years. Phoebe wanted to talk to me about it, but I don't want to bother her. She's supposed to be having the best time of her life right now with Shade. They seem so happy, and the last thing she needs is listening to my problems."

Celise nodded. "I understand, but you can talk to me. You won't ruin my mood."

Faye smirked. "Yes, I will, because I just gave you a better one."

"No, I promise. Besides, I see something's on your mind."

Faye sighed. "Very well." She took a deep breath as if to prepare herself. "Ever since we left that house, I've been thinking about Silver. I didn't mean to bind him to me. I didn't believe what Nightmare told me, that you can bind a Fighter to you from a single intimate touch, but when they started beating up Shade, I had to do something, and it sure got their attention." She bit her lip. "Silver's eyes flashed once, and it didn't take long before he completely lost it. He tried to finish the bonding, but the Fighters stopped him. I have no idea where he's now, but Jade told me he's probably in a lot of pain. That really makes me feel bad."

Celise felt sorry for Faye, but she felt sorry for Silver, too. He had to be in a lot of pain. His eyes had to flash two more times to seal the bond, and without Faye, that was impossible. Until Faye was able to bind him to her, his bond would scream for her in the worst kind of way, slowly torment him out of his mind. "So what are you going to do?"

"There's nothing I can do. I have no idea where the Fighters live. I can't go to Silver."

Celise leaned closer. "Remember the signal I used to track Nightmare? I could use it again to find Silver."

Faye gasped. Horror filled her gaze. "No! Don't do that. If you do, who knows what will happen. All I want is to find a way *out* of this. Sure, he's hot as hell, but I don't want to be his bound one. I wouldn't mind doing him, but if that results in a bond, then no thank you."

"You have to do *something*, Faye."

She raised her hands, with her palms out. "I know, I

41

know. I just don't know what ... yet. I need to think."

Celise nodded. She understood. Pressing Faye further would do no good, but sooner or later, she'd have to deal with the situation.

CHAPTER 5

Celise's heart thundered hard as she knocked on Wind's and Diane's door the following day at noon. She assumed Jade was already there judging by the familiar car in the driveway.

She'd never been this nervous in her entire life. Her body shook, her head spun, and her breathing was strained. She could barely stand still when she caught someone approaching the door from the inside.

Celise had made up her mind.

She'd become Wind's bound one because she loved him. He didn't love her now, but once the bond was hers, he would. What happened after that, only time could tell.

Celise took a deep breath as the door opened. She looked straight into Wind's shining eyes.

He was dressed in jeans and a black shirt, without any paint stains this time.

When he saw her, he gave her that gentle smile she loved so much. It always made her feel safe when his calm and gentleness radiated at her.

He took a slow step closer. Even if he was smiling, there was an underlying worry in his eyes. It was almost as if he worried *she'd* turn around and run away. He grabbed her hand.

Wind's touch sent goosebumps all over her skin.

"I'm glad you came, Celise."

Her nerves made it difficult to relax. It made it even more of a feat to maintain eye contact with him. She didn't want him to see or sense how freaked out she was. "I've come to a decision." Her voice had come out a croak, and her face heated.

He tensed, and in a way, she found it sweet. Maybe he cared more about her than he dared to admit.

"Are you here to tell me you don't want to be with me?"

"Do you believe that?" she whispered.

He hesitated. "I'm having a hard time reading you, and that's something I'm usually good at. It's an ability Diane gave me since she's always found it difficult."

Celise nodded. That was why she hadn't been able to hide her feelings from him, but then again, she hadn't really been able to hide them from anyone.

She'd had a conversation with Wind a few years ago about her feelings for him. He'd been kind and gentle when he'd told her they could never be. It'd hurt like hell, but he'd been understanding and had remained her friend.

"And what are you reading?" she asked.

"You look both happy and sad."

She nodded. That was spot on. She was happy about her decision, but it meant she had to take him from Diane. Not to mention her friend wouldn't be with them much longer.

She grabbed his hand, gently caressing the back of his hand with her thumb. His skin was smooth and warm. The touch awakened a hunger within her she had a hard time controlling. She wanted to throw herself at him, and stay in his arms forever.

Wind tensed.

She met his gaze. "Does this hurt you?"

"Not physically, but my bond protests because it's an intimate touch. If we'd shaken hands, I wouldn't have felt a thing, but my bond knows you're a threat."

Celise frowned. "A threat?"

He shrugged. "You know what I mean."

She took a deep breath. "I've studied cyborgs for years, but I intentionally avoided studying how to transfer the bond to a new bound one. I'm not saying I didn't peak at it, but I didn't put too much effort into it."

"Because of me." His voice was filled with understanding.

"Yes, because of you."

Silence lingered between them as they looked into each other's eyes.

Wind's grip on her hand tightened. "You didn't answer my question, Celise." The worry in his eyes radiated.

She wished she could hold him, but didn't want to bring him more discomfort. Celise let go of his hand. "Do you still want me to become your bound one?"

"Yes. Very much so."

"Are you sure? I mean, there's no guaranty things will work between us."

He took a step closer. "I'm sure. I prefer you over any other woman MedAct would introduce me to."

She closed her eyes, grimacing. "Be really, really sure, Wind. It will devastate me if you change your mind."

Without warning, he wrapped his arms around her.

Celise couldn't stop her gasp when his body heat surrounded her. Being this close to him gave her an inner peace she rarely felt. She couldn't help but rest her head on his shoulder, even if it most likely made his bond protest. He didn't smell like paint today. Instead, her nose was filled with a light, but masculine scent she instantly fell in love with.

"I won't change my mind," he said. "I promise I'll do everything in my power to make this work."

CHAPTER 6

Wind had no idea *how* he was going to make things work between them, but he had to convince Celise she'd made the right decision. He'd been worried she'd turn him down, but she was an intelligent woman.

She knew well why he wasn't capable of stronger feelings for her, and maybe she'd chosen to accept that.

Celise smelled nice. She had that vanilla perfume on again, but his bond hated what he was doing. Everything inside him told him to release her, stop touching her, stop cheating on Diane, even if he, deep down, knew he wasn't.

Wind wished the bond could understand that. The discomfort, the heartache, and the stress made him want to scream, but he remained silent. Too much was at stake.

She pulled away and gave him a shy smile.

Strangely, there was a small part of him that didn't want to let go.

"Maybe it's best if you don't touch me right now. I see what it does to you," she said.

He blinked. "You don't want me to hold you?"

"I do, but your bond doesn't want you to, and since we don't know how to transfer it to me yet, there's no point in tormenting you."

He gasped when his bond responded to her words. It was as if it felt gratitude toward her understanding, but only for a split second. Yet, Wind had a strong feeling he'd be able to hold her now without the bond going crazy. His heart kicked up speed as he reached for her again. He had to find out ...

"I'm glad you could come, Celise," Diane said from somewhere behind him.

He winced and lowered his arms. He glanced at his love as Diane approached from the living room.

She smiled, but her eyes were tired. Her skin was pale, and she looked fragile as she supported herself on a cane. It was impossible to miss that she was sick, reminding him of the present situation. His heart ached from the knowledge of what was to come.

Wind clenched his jaws together to stop himself from becoming emotional. He'd cried many times in her arms by now, but more tears wouldn't change anything.

He was going to lose her.

It was just a matter of time.

His gaze turned to Jade Silva, who stood next to Diane. The doctor was a sweet-looking woman with soft features, but her brown eyes were filled with so much strength and determination, it almost made him gasp. This woman was not someone to play around with.

Diane hugged Celise. "Thank you for coming, my friend. It means the world to me."

Celise smiled but seemed unable to answer.

Jade approached and shook her hand. "Hello, Celise. It's nice to see you again. How's your work with the cyborgs here in Glaswell coming along for you?"

She appeared to take a deep breath, as if she was trying to relax. "Great. I learn more and more each day."

"And what do the cyborgs think about your work?"

"No one is complaining so far."

The doctor nodded. "They trust you. That's good. Gaining a cyborg's trust is not easy."

"I've noticed. Some of them didn't even want to talk to me in the beginning."

Wind clenched his knuckles. The thought of other cyborgs touching Celise filled him with a pinch of anger. It was her job, but still, it didn't rub him the right way.

He stilled when realization hit him.

Yesterday, he couldn't even see himself being bound to her, and now, he was reacting like this?

Jade turned to him. "What do you think, Wind? Is

Celise doing a good job?"

He cleared his throat, trying to get rid of the sudden emotions. "She's always thorough when she examines me."

The doctor grinned and her gaze darkened. "She's probably just as thorough when she examines other cyborgs, don't you think?"

Wind frowned. The image Jade planted inside his mind didn't sit well with him at all. "Are you implying something?"

She only kept grinning and headed to the living room.

CHAPTER 7

Celise followed Jade with a thundering heart.

Wind and Diane held hands as they also headed toward the room.

The sight hit her in the chest. She had to remind herself he wasn't hers yet. Besides, they deserved last moments together, because after today, everything would change.

With trembling hands and weak knees, she sat on one of the couches inside the big bright living room. A round table stood in the middle.

Diane and Wind sat on the other couch while Jade sat next to Celise and took a tablet out of her bag.

Celise tried to stay calm. She avoided looking at Wind and Diane but felt their eyes on her. It made her feel like she stood on a huge stage. She didn't like that. She'd never liked that.

Jade glanced over all of them. "Before we begin, I want to make sure everyone has agreed to this, and that there's no doubt whatsoever. I don't want to waste your time, and I don't want to waste mine."

"I'm sure," Diane said. "There's no one better suited to take my place than Celise."

Emotions washed over Celise, a huge mix of everything from pure joy to insecurity. Her life had taken an unexpected turn, and handling it seemed almost impossible. What if she was dreaming? Would she wake up soon?

Celise clenched her fists. No, this was all real.

Frightening real, and yet, exciting.

"I'm sure, too," Wind said.

Jade turned to her. "Are you, Celise?"

She swallowed and nodded. She couldn't help but glimpse at Wind. "Yes."

The doctor studied her. "You don't look sure."

She winced. "I'm just nervous."

Jade took a breath. "Yes, I guess you should be." She tapped on the tablet's screen, and silence filled the room.

Celise remembered a few years back when she'd told Wind about her feelings for him, but only after he'd figured it out and asked. It'd been the most embarrassing day of her life. He'd been kind and understanding, and despite him telling he'd always be her friend, she'd stayed away from him for *weeks* after that.

It had been *him*, who'd finally taken contact. They'd gone for a walk and talked about anything on their minds, but after that day, being close to Wind had become too difficult.

She'd always smiled, always been kind, doing everything to maintain their friendship, but on the inside, she'd been slowly dying. That had been her reality for so long.

Now, here she was, making a life changing decision she'd never seen coming.

"I assume you all know about the responsibilities," Jade said, "but I have to go through it, anyway. I need to know you understand what you're getting yourselves into." She placed the tablet on the table. The screen glowed in different shades of blue. "Everything we say from now will be recorded. It will be your contract with MedAct."

They all nodded.

"Very well. Let's begin." She turned to Celise. "Please place your hand on the tablet."

A gentle light came from the screen as she touched it. She pulled away a few seconds later, when the light disappeared. She gazed at Wind. Sadness lingered in his beautiful aluminum, shiny eyes. It made her hold her breath. She couldn't get away from the feeling that she was forcing him into this. He didn't want her. She understood why, but it didn't lessen the ache in her chest.

Jade took a deep breath. "I, Doctor Jade Silva, hereby open the contract between Diane Wright and Celise Campbell regarding the cyborg Wind, who was created and awakened by MedAct fifteen years ago. Wind is bound to Diane Wright, but Diane is dying, and therefore, Wind needs a new bound one. Both Diane Wright and Wind agrees to that Celise Campbell takes Diane's place." The doctor looked at Celise. "There's no way out of this contract. Only death can release you from it. Mistreating Wind in any way is punishable, and you'll be supervised the first two years during your time with him. Do you understand?"

Celise took an unsteady breath. "I understand."

"Good. Now confirm you desire this."

She touched the tablet again, this time with a shaky hand. "I, Celise Campbell confirm that I want to become Wind's new bound one. I'll take care of him and cherish him the way a bound one should." She gazed at Wind again.

His face was tense, his eyes set on her as he held Diane's hand in his with a grim expression. He was about to lose the most important person in his life, and she could barely imagine what he was going through.

"Diane, your turn." Jade handed her the tablet.

There were tears in Diane's eyes as she placed her hand on the tablet. Her voice shook when she spoke. "I, Diane Wright, agree to—" She remained silent for a while. Her reluctance was written all over her face. "I, Diane Wright, agree to that Celise Campbell becomes Wind's new—" She looked at Celise with a horror-filled gaze.

There was nothing Celise could say or do to make Diane feel better, but she could give her a smile filled with promises. She'd already promised Wind would be safe, that he'd be taken care of, and that he'd always be loved. It was a promise stronger than any contract MedAct could ever write.

"I'm sorry." Diane relaxed and dried her tears. She straightened her back. "I accept Celise Campbell as Wind's new bound one." She pulled her hand from the tablet.

"You too, Wind," Jade said.

He nodded and took a deep breath before he let go of Diane's hand and reached for the tablet. He froze with his hand on it, just staring at it for a while.

Celise didn't miss the confusion that suddenly radiated from his eyes, but when he leaned forward and groaned as if in pain, she tensed. Worry filled every part of her body.

Something wasn't right.

"I know it hurts," Jade said, "but the pain you feel now

will subside as soon as you confirm the contract. Don't prolong it."

Celise wanted to tell him to stop, that he didn't have to do this, that he could stay with Diane. She didn't want to see him like this. She didn't want to be the cause of his pain.

"I, Wind ... bound to Diane Wright—" He groaned again, unable to go on. He shook his head as if he was trying to get rid of the pain.

Diane looked terrified. She held her hands over her mouth as tears ran down her cheeks. "Wind ..." She reached for him.

The doctor raised her hand. "Don't."

Diane froze, and with resignation in her eyes, pulled back.

"Finish, Wind," Jade ordered.

His voice quivered. "I accept ... I ... accept Celise ... as my new ... bound one."

Before Celise could relax, Wind let out a gut-wrenching cry. He threw himself off the sofa, writhing on the floor. He curled in a fetal position with his hands against his chest. His body trembled, his throat and face turned bright red as a thin coat of sweat broke out on his skin.

Celise and Diane both flew from their seats. "Wind!" they yelled at the same time.

Jade raised her hand again, commanding attention. "Don't go near him! He'll accidently hurt you if you do. He's not able to control his reactions right now."

Seeing Wind like this made it difficult for Celise to stand by and do nothing. The way he twisted on the floor told her he could break bones with his strength. When he grabbed the table leg and squeezed, the wood cracked. It sent chills down her spine. Cyborgs were strong, a lot stronger than humans, and he'd just proven that.

"You said his pain would go away once he agreed to the contract!" Diane yelled at Jade.

"I lied."

Disbelief shone in her eyes. "What? Why?"

"Because it would've made him hesitate. He would've chosen to die with you. His bond is fighting against his decision. It's trying to stop him, but if he gets through this, one huge obstacle will be behind you all."

"What do you mean *if*?" Anger surged through Celise. She couldn't believe Jade hadn't been honest.

"There's a slight chance his bond won't accept his decision, that it's unable to make the transfer."

She gasped. "What will happen then?"

Jade remained silent, but her chest heaved as if she'd taken a breath.

The sound of cracking wood filled the room again

when Wind squeezed the poor table leg even more. Celise winced, unable to escape the feeling as if something had cracked inside *her*, too.

"He'll die," Jade said.

Diane burst into hysterical sobs.

Celise reacted instantly. She ran up to Diane and wrapped her arms around Wind's bound one as she cried against her shoulder.

Celise wanted nothing more but run up to Wind too, hold him, and tell him everything would be all right. He just had to hang on for a little bit longer, and it'd be over soon, but when she looked at him, she saw no improvement. Fear skittered down her spine.

He screamed and tremored, and finally snapped the table leg off. The table swayed but didn't fall over. The other three held it up.

"You should've told us," Celise snapped.

"Then you would've never gone through with this, and Wind would've died anyway when Diane—" Jade paused. "You don't have to worry, Diane. Neither do you, Celise. It's rare that a cyborg dies at this stage. During all the years I've been working at MedAct, it has only happened twice."

Diane didn't say anything. She tried to dry her eyes, but the tears kept coming.

"How often do you do this?" Celise asked. "How often

does a cyborg change his bound one?"

"It happens more often than you think. Humans don't live as long as cyborgs do, as you know, so at least a few times each year. None of them want to become a Fighter, so they agree to switch their bound one before it's too late. But sometimes, the bound ones dies unexpectedly, and those who survive, join the Fighters."

Eventually, Wind stopped screaming, but his pain was still obvious. He kept shaking and groaning with ragged breaths. His eyes were closed, and he seemed swept away in his own mind.

"It's over soon." Jade's voice was gentle, comforting.

No one spoke as the minutes passed, and after what felt like an eternity, Wind finally exhaled and relaxed. Sweat covered his body, exhaustion radiated from him, but his breathing slowly calmed.

Diane was instantly at his side. She wrapped her arms around him as more tears ran down her cheeks. Equal parts joy and worry shone on her face.

Celise remained where she stood. Wind wasn't hers yet, even if she officially was his bound one now. She tried to convince herself it was the right thing to do, taking over the bond. Without her, Wind would, one way or another, die but when she saw the pain it caused them, she couldn't help but think twice. Trying to tell herself she was saving him became more and more difficult to believe.

Wind lay still in Diane's arms. His eyes were closed, his mouth slightly open, and he seemed completely drained. He remained like that for a while as he regained his strength.

Then he opened his eyes and met her gaze.

Celise held her breath.

His eyes were bright and intense. There was a determination she'd never seen before, and there was also something new. Something she'd never expected to see in his eyes.

Interest.

And it was directed *at* her ...

CHAPTER 8

"How are you feeling?" Diane asked Wind when they'd reseated themselves. She held his hand in hers as if she was trying to comfort him, but he didn't seem to notice.

Exhaustion shone in his shining eyes. "Like I've been hit by a truck." His usually gentle gaze shot to Jade and darkened. "You should've told me about the pain. I have the right to choose my own fate."

"Yes, you do, and you chose Celise," Jade answered. "What you felt now was nothing compared to what you would've felt if you'd survived Diane's death without being bound to Celise."

"You can't know for sure it would've affected my decision," he growled.

"All cyborgs who've been told have chosen death."

Wind didn't seem happy, and Celise didn't blame him. She was angry as well, but Diane seemed mostly happy that Wind had survived.

"Can you tell us what you felt?" Celise asked.

Wind turned his gaze at her, and she winced when his anger didn't subside. She couldn't help but wonder if it was directed at her now. After all, it was *her* fault he'd experienced pain. *She* was the cause of it.

"Nothing new. The bond protested, but I've never felt it fight the way it did. The moment I said I accept you as my bound one, it went completely crazy."

"But you feel no pain now when you said you accept me, right?"

Realization seemed to hit him. "No, I didn't." He exhaled. "Thank God." His last words were merely a whisper.

"You won't experience that again," Jade said. "Your bond hasn't accepted Celise yet, so this is far from over, but the pain you felt a few minutes ago will never go through your system again. That you survived proves your bond is willing to make the transfer. You have to work together to make it happen. All *three* of you."

"What do you mean?" Diane asked.

"Throwing Wind at Celise won't work. The bond must choose her willingly. You must give it a reason to want her."

Wind frowned. "You mean, show the bond that Celise is better than Diane?"

Jade nodded. "Exactly."

He reared back against the fabric of the couch. "But, she isn't."

Agony surged through Celise. She lowered her gaze and tried not to show how much it hurt.

"Oh, my God," Wind said with horror in his eyes. "I didn't mean it like that, Celise."

"Don't worry about it." She avoided looking at him as the tension in the room grew.

Jade stood. "Well, as you see, you still have a lot to work with. Just like with the Fighters, Wind's eyes have to flash three times. It'll be difficult to get the first flash, but once it happens, it'll be easier to get the second and the third."

Celise dared to look at him. His gaze was set on her, and the underlying seriousness there made her hold her breath. He truly regretted what he'd said. He hadn't meant it. It was written all over his face, and it eased her tension.

"And how do we achieve that?" Diane asked.

"There are several ways, but what's most important is that you and Wind stop touching each other. If you do, it'll become easier for his bond to make the transfer."

Agony hit Celise in the chest again, and she bit her lower lip to stop herself from bursting into tears. She could almost feel Diane's pain as her own when she saw the shock in her tired eyes. "Diane, I ..."

Diane wiped away a tear and gave her a trembling

but reassuring smile before turning to Jade. Resignation lingered in her expression. "I understand."

"One way to get that first flash is to fool the bond," Jade said.

"How?" Celise regretted not studying the bond. It would've helped them a lot if she'd known how to proceed without having to ask Jade every question.

"Make the bond think it touches Diane. You can do that by playing a kissing game."

Wind jerked into a sitting position. He seemed to feel better, which Celise was thankful for, but the look on his face said he wasn't interested in any kissing games.

"What kind of kissing game?" Diane asked.

"Tie a cloth around Wind's eyes, and then take turns kissing him. That way, the bond can't determine who's kissing him. Once he's aroused enough, you remove the cloth, and the bond should be more willing to comply. It might work the first time, it might work on the tenth time. It's different for every cyborg. Remember that."

Heat rushed to Celise's face. The thought of kissing him, to actually do it without it being wrong made her hope the kissing game would take place.

Even if Wind didn't seem thrilled, Diane was more difficult to read. She wasn't crying anymore, her expression was calm, but Celise still had a hard time to determine what Diane thought about the doctor's words.

"Listen," Jade said. "I understand what this sounds like, but you all must do everything in your power. You must work together, and that means trying every single thing you can come up with."

Celise gulped. "You mean—"

Jade nodded. "Yes. A threesome is one of the things on the list. When I said you must do everything in your power, I meant *everything*. Literally. Do you understand?" Her eyes rested on each of them with a serious gaze.

Celise exchanged surprised glances with Diane and Wind. She'd expected this process to be difficult, but she'd never thought they'd have to take things *that* far. Hopefully, they wouldn't have to.

"This is all about intimacy," the doctor went on. "Wind must get used to your touch, Celise. His bond must *accept* your touch. Once it does, you should be able to sleep with him to make the first flash happen."

She'd barely dared to imagine what it'd be like to have sex with Wind, and now, she'd soon be able to experience it for real. The thought of it made her body heat rise.

"Remember, this is a matter of life or death. You've no idea how much time you have to make the transfer. If you're lucky, it will only take a few days, but we've had couples where it took months, so don't waste your time. If the bond isn't fully transferred, and Diane dies, Wind might die as well. You need those three flashes. Two are not enough, and one will take you nowhere."

Jade's voice was firm and her words hard to listen to, but she was right. Wind and Diane seemed to agree, even if discomfort lingered in their eyes.

"Celise, you'll also move in with Diane and Wind today, or they move in with you."

She winced and stared at the doctor. Celise opened her mouth, but no words came.

Jade turned to Diane and Wind. "You two, from now on, you only touch if it's really necessary."

Their expressions were tense, and Diane, who still held Wind's hand in hers, slowly pulled away. Her fingers trembled. The pain written all over her face was unmistakable.

"One last thing," Jade said, as if unaffected by Diane's sorrow, and locked her gaze at Wind. "You might end up in a transition phase once your eyes flash for the first time. It doesn't happen to all cyborgs who go through this, but some end up being bound to both women until the last flash happens."

His eyes widened, and his jaw dropped. "How's that even possible?"

"It's possible because your bond to Diane won't disappear until your bond to Celise is fully in place."

He frowned. "Won't that make it more difficult to become bound to Celise?"

"It will, so let's hope your bond to Diane disappears with the first flash, but I'm telling you all, just in case. A comfort is, it's rare, but it does happen."

Wind sighed and nodded. "I understand. What will happen when my bond to Diane is gone? Will I forget her?"

"No. Your feelings for Diane will always be there. They are real. When Diane dies, you'll feel the same pain everyone feels when they lose a loved one, but you won't die with her." She picked up her tablet and pushed on the digital buttons a few times. "The contract is now sealed. Wind, you're now officially bound to Celise."

He clenched his fists. "What if we don't succeed?"

Jade's hand froze over the device. Her expression expressionless. "Then you'll die."

CHAPTER 9

"Are you sure about this?" Wind looked at Celise, where she stood by the open front door, throwing her bag over her shoulder. Through the door, he noticed Jade driving away.

She gave him a gentle smile. "I'm sure. You don't have to come with me to my place. I'll just pick up a few things, and be back soon. I'm going to need some clothing, my toothbrush, and other things if I'm supposed to live here for a while. Besides, Diane needs you right now. This is your last chance to ... to be together ..."

"I'm bound to you now. I should go with you." Saying those words made his bond protest, and all he wanted was to go back to Diane and forget this was happening. At least it didn't make him feel sick to think or say he was bound to Celise anymore.

She stilled. "Only on paper."

Wind didn't reply. Instead, he looked toward the living room, where Diane sat, and just the thought of her warmed his heart.

"I can't help but think I'm doing something wrong." Celise's voice was barely a whisper.

His gaze returned to Celise. "What do you mean?"

"You want nothing more but to be with Diane. I see the longing in your eyes, and here I am, taking you away from her."

Wind grabbed her hand. "You have no idea how difficult it is to say this, but I *have* to. The three of us must move beyond those kind of thoughts if we want to make this work. Yes, the bond is protesting like crazy. Yes, you're taking me away from Diane, but don't let those feelings rule you. We're all doing this because we have to. Our fates are sealed. The contract is signed. I'm yours now. We have no other way to go but forward."

Celise blinked and stared at him with wide eyes. "I thought you didn't want this."

"I want to die with Diane, but I also want to live." He sighed. "I'm a little bit messed up right now." He caressed the back of her hand with his thumb. Hers was tiny compared to his. It looked so fragile and gentle with long fingers and slim palm. "Jade has given us plenty of ideas. I think we should try them."

"The kissing game." Her cheeks turned pink.

Wind couldn't help but smile. Strangely enough, the idea started to appeal to him more and more. "Yes, the kissing game."

She cleared her throat. "Jade said we have to do everything in our power to make this work."

"She did, but I worry my bond will turn on the primitive instincts that rule every newborn cyborg."

Celise pulled her hand back, her cheek trembled. "You believe you'll want to protect Diane from me."

"Yes. Jade didn't say anything about it, but it has crossed my mind a few times."

She took a shaky breath, and her gaze darkened. "I guess there's only one way to find out."

He didn't like the sudden coldness in her voice, but he understood. His words had hurt her ... again. It was written all over her face as she dried away a tear. He was becoming an expert on that lately.

"I need to go. I'll be back within the hour. Don't waste it." She stormed through the open front door.

Wind didn't move from his spot as he watched her drive away. He'd never meant to hurt her, but his bond didn't allow him to be on the usual friendly terms with her anymore. Instead, it made him edgy, and overprotective of Diane. He, who usually never raised his voice, was in defense mode.

70

It sure was a messed up situation.

Wind closed the door and went back to the living room.

Diane sat where he'd left her. She was crying again. Her eyes were red and swollen, and he wanted nothing more but to hold her. He wanted to tell her everything was going to be all right, but it would be a lie.

Nothing was going to be all right.

Once Celise returned, he'd show her to her room, and they would initiate the process of making her his bound one.

Diane dried her eyes with a tissue as he entered the room.

Wind sat by her side but didn't touch her. He remembered Jade's words.

She gave him a gentle smile. "I'm trying to tell myself, over and over again, we did the right thing, but it hurts more than I thought it would. At least, now I know you'll be safe when I die."

Wind lowered his head. "You should let me die with you."

Diane gasped. "Never. That would be selfish of me, and what if you'd survive my death?"

He clenched his jaw. "Most cyborgs die when their bound one dies."

"I'm not willing to risk it. Besides, the contract is

71

already signed. Celise is your bound one now. She loves you, and I know she'll take good care of you. I know you two will take good care of each other. I just wish—"

Wind couldn't hold back the need to touch her anymore. He placed his hand on hers. "Wish what?"

She gave him another smile. "I just wish I could have you by my side until the very end."

He pushed the damaged table away and placed himself on his knees in front of her. "I just told Celise that we must look beyond our emotions; that we must be professional about this, but I don't know if I can. I don't want this, Diane." He laid his head on her legs. "I'm so torn. One second, I've accepted this, and the next, I feel like this. Everything protests within me." Wind felt Diane's hand on his head.

She pulled her fingers through his hair.

Her touch was bliss, and it calmed his chaotic emotions.

"Have your feelings changed toward her since all this began?"

He hesitated. "There was a moment in the hallway, when she and I spoke, it felt like the bond had slightly accepted her. It was as if it allowed her to come a little bit closer."

"That sounds like progress." She dried her eyes yet again with a handkerchief. "I have stopped crying now. The ache in my heart will never go away, and I'll miss you like crazy, but you're right. We must handle this professionally. Your life is at stake, and I refuse to let you die with me."

Her words filled him with pain he couldn't ignore. It meant he wouldn't be allowed to touch her ... ever again ... "Celise told me she'd be back within an hour. She also told me not to waste it." Wind sat up on the couch again. "Let me hold you one last time."

Diane moved closer and nodded.

Wind wrapped his arms around her. He closed his eyes and took an unsteady breath.

A new chapter in his life was about to begin ...

... and another was closing.

CHAPTER 10

Everything still felt strange and surreal as Celise parked her car outside Wind's and Diane's home a second time this day. She looked at the huge villa and could barely believe what was about to begin.

She'd imagined being Wind's bound one so many times, but it had always been just a fantasy. She'd never dared to believe it would actually come true.

He was bound to her now, according to the contract, and that was even more surreal. It would take some time getting used to.

It didn't feel like he was bound to her, though. He'd been insensitive toward her, and that hurt. Celise understood why, but she wasn't doing anything wrong. At least, she tried to tell herself that, but he'd made her feel like she was guilty of a crime. It was definitely not a good base to start a relationship on.

And what if he'd snap and try to defend Diane? Would he hurt her?

Celise shook her head. No, he wouldn't do that. She'd known Wind for several years, and she trusted him. He'd always been kind. He'd never treated her badly because of her feelings for him, and she'd always be grateful for that. His behavior these past few hours was a new side of him she'd never seen before. She couldn't expect him to be his usual self, considering the situation, but she hoped it'd go away once everything was over.

Celise prepared herself and stepped out of the car. It was time to face her future, and all she could do was pray it'd end well.

She grabbed her bag and threw it over her shoulder. It was packed with everything she'd need. It was everything from clothes to cosmetics, but she hadn't taken any of her books. She doubted she'd have time to read.

Celise knocked on the door, and a short minute later, Wind opened it.

Their gazes met, and silence filled the hallway.

Celise couldn't help but take in his beauty as they watched each other. He wasn't as tall as Shade, but almost a head taller than her. His broad shoulders, muscular arms, and fit body flushed her with a tingling feeling all over.

She had no idea what to do, or say, but Wind seemed calmer now. His shining eyes had always mesmerized her. The wisdom, kindness, and gentleness she'd always seen in them was there, but also something else.

He seemed amused for some reason.

That was rather surprising.

"Why are you looking at me like that?" she asked.

His lips twitched. "I find your insecurity rather cute."

Celise winced. "What?" That was the last thing she'd expected him to say.

He took a step closer, and she held her breath.

Wind grabbed her hands. "I want to try something. Is that all right?"

Celise swallowed. "Depends on what it is."

"I want to kiss you."

She gasped.

Wind took another step closer, and when he wrapped his arms around her, she feared her heart might burst. It was beating so hard and fast it almost hurt.

Celise placed her hands against his chest and stopped his progress. "Wait." She took a deep breath in a meaningless attempt to calm herself. "Won't that hurt you?

"That's what I want to find out. Things have changed since yesterday."

She squeaked when he grabbed her neck and, without warning, pressed his lips to hers. He didn't give her time

76

to react before he opened her mouth with his and pushed his tongue inside.

His grip on her neck was like solid rock. She'd never experienced his strength first hand, but now, it slowly sank in how strong he really was. She'd seen him snap the wooden table leg, but to actually experience it physically was a completely different thing.

There was no way for her to get away.

Not that she wanted to.

Wind held her in place. All Celise could do was put her hands on his strong arms, and tag along.

She couldn't help but wonder if this behavior was because of the bond transfer, but the more his mouth tasted hers, the less she cared. Heat traveled to her sex, dizziness filled her head, fogging her mind, and she slowly sank deeper and deeper into the sweet pleasures his mouth gave her.

She starved for his touch, and when he gave it to her willingly, Celise was ready to give in completely to get what her body so badly longed for.

Wind jerked away with a loud groan, much too soon. He leaned forward, grimacing, and pressing his hands to his chest.

Guilt filled her. She should've known better. "I'm so sorry." Touching her had hurt him ... again.

He gave her a stiff smile. "Don't worry. I wanted to see

77

if something had changed, but I guess I was wrong." He took a deep breath, straightening his back as he relaxed. The pain appeared to wash off him.

Celise's turned her head when she noticed movement in the corner of her eye.

Diane stood near the entrance door to the living room, watching them.

Ice slid down Celise's spine, and she froze in place, gasping.

Diane had seen everything.

"What did it feel like this time?" Diane asked Wind as she joined them.

Wind smiled. "It wasn't as painful as before, and I was able to kiss her for at least two seconds longer than last time."

She stopped by his side. "Did it turn you on?"

He remained silent for a while. "No."

Diane only nodded.

Celise entered the house and closed the door behind her. She tried to ignore her arousal and their conversation, but it was difficult. Her touch maybe didn't affect him, but his sure affected her. She wanted nothing more but throw herself at Wind and finish what he'd started.

"Wind and I've been talking," Diane said. "We've come up with a plan."

Celise licked her lips. She could still taste Wind on

them. "What kind of plan?"

Diane seemed to feel better judging by her gentle smile. Her eyes were still red from all the crying, though. "The day is coming to an end, but before we go to sleep, we thought it'd be a good idea to try out Jade's suggestion."

Celise gulped. "Which suggestion?"

"The kissing game. The sooner, the better. We have to fool the bond into thinking it's all right to kiss you."

"I thought it might work without the kissing game," Wind said. "That's why I kissed you now, but it didn't."

Celise could only nod. Her head was already spinning from all this.

"I have a feeling we have to play the game a few times," Diane said.

"A few times?" It sent her heart into a frenzy. A few times meant constant arousal from his touch. That was a disaster! He wouldn't feel a thing, but it would slowly push her out of her mind until she'd reach a point where she'd be unable to handle it.

"Yes, until I feel a change, some kind of improvement. If my bond can accept us kissing, I should be able to move forward after that."

She tightened her fists, trying to hide her chaotic emotions. "I understand."

"Oh, and another thing," Diane said.

Celise tightened her fists until her nails bit into her

palms. "What?"

"We thought it'd be a good idea if you and Wind sleep in the same bed from now on."

CHAPTER 11

Celise couldn't believe she was unpacking her things into Diane's and Wind's wardrobe. As if that wasn't enough, Diane had decided she and Wind would share *their* bedroom. The bedroom they'd slept in for fifteen years.

She glanced at the huge king-sized bed as she put her shirts away. It could easily fit three people. The white linens were fresh, and it looked inviting with its fluffy pillows and cozy comforter. She didn't doubt it was comfortable to sleep in ... or do other things in.

An image of her, Wind, and Diane naked together on those white sheets, playing and caressing each other entered her mind when she remembered Jade's suggestion of a threesome.

Celise shivered and averted her eyes, pushing the thought away; didn't want to think about it. Instead, she grabbed her pants from the bag, but when two hands suddenly grabbed her by the waist, she squeaked and dropped them.

"Don't be afraid," Wind whispered in her ear.

She froze in place, just staring ahead with a pounding heart as his big hands gently, but firmly traveled toward her stomach. A gasp left her lips when they slid under her T-shirt, touching her bare skin. "What are you doing?" she asked. His touch shot a wave of arousal through her, but the thought of him pulling away lingered in the back of her mind. Any second now, he'd leave her frustrated and wanting.

"I'm feeling you. I figured I'll have to do this a lot for my bond to accept you."

She held her breath when his fingers slipped down her pants. "This is torture."

His hand stilled. "It's not my intention to hurt you. I'm just trying to make my eyes flash."

She understood, but for her, it meant a lot of touching with no satisfaction, as long as he didn't feel anything. She doubted *he* understood that. "And is it working?" Her voice was barely a whisper.

He leaned closer her ear, gently nipping the tip with his lips.

She couldn't stop another gasp from the unexpected touch. Weakness filled her knees, need grew greater.

"No, but it doesn't hurt touching you anymore. My bond is still protesting, though, but this is progress."

Celise rested her head against his broad shoulder and closed her eyes as he kept exploring her stomach. "You feel nothing? Nothing at all?" She tensed but refused to let it hurt, whatever his answer would be.

Wind was silent for a while. "This doesn't arouse me if that's what you're wondering." His voice lowered to a whisper. "But it arouses *you*."

Blood rushed to her face. No words were able to leave her mouth.

"You're easy to read, Celise. You've been aroused all day. I might not be able to do anything about it yet, but I promise you, as soon as my bond is all right with it, I'll make you feel good. *Really* good."

Her knees gave finally in beneath her, and she would've landed on the floor if he hadn't been holding her.

A chuckle came from behind them.

"You're bringing the poor girl to her breaking point, Wind. I doubt you'll be able to stop her from jumping you if you keep talking like that," Diane said from the other side of the room.

Celise jerked away and spun around when she heard the female voice, then stared right into Diane's eyes. Shame flooded her.

Diane had heard and seen everything ... again!

Desperately, she tried to shake the lustful haze Wind had put her in. It was almost painful, but she had to do it. The last thing she wanted was Diane seeing her like this.

Her friend's eyes were filled with understanding as she came closer. "Don't worry, Celise. This is what we have to do to transfer the bond, isn't it?" She waved a piece of cloth in front of her, and a grin spread across her face. "Since Wind is so tall, he can sit on the stool. It will be easier for us to kiss him. What do you think?"

She grabbed the stool that stood next to the closet and placed it in the middle of the floor.

Wind sat and took the cloth from Diane, gave them both one last look, and tied it around his head, covering his eyes. When he was done, he lowered his arms, took a deep breath, and waited.

Celise swallowed. Her heart refused to calm. "Now what?"

Diane's face lit up. "Now, we begin."

Next to the bed on the wall hung a wireless player, no bigger than a small book. Diane waved her hand in front of it and it turned on with a few blue lights on the digital screen. Diane touched the screen, and seconds later, slow and romantic music began to play. Then she pushed a switch on the wall, and a gentle light filled the room.

Wind was still not moving or speaking, but his chest heaved faster, and he clenched his fists.

Celise watched him. Was he nervous? Or was this turning him on? She couldn't tell, but maybe, it was a mix of both. After all, Diane was about to touch him. That had to awaken his interest.

She just wished his interest would awaken from *her* touch as well.

Diane placed her hands on his arm.

He inhaled deeply and licked his lips.

Would he be able to tell who was touching him with the blindfold on? Celise thought so. After all these years, he should be able to recognize Diane's touch, and besides, he was a cyborg. His senses were more heightened than a human's. If that was the case, this game was pointless.

Diane's hands glided up his arm and continued over his chest, gently and sensually caressing one of his nipples over his shirt before continuing.

His lips parted, and he tilted his head back as a silent groan left his mouth.

The sight was the most erotic thing Celise had ever seen. Her hands shook, her chest heaved with every deep breath. Would she ever be able to touch him without giving away it was her?

Wind's lips twitched when Diane unbuttoned his shirt. He straightened his back and pushed his chest slightly forward, inviting the touch.

Diane's hand grazed his naked skin, and all Celise

could do was stare. It mesmerized her, almost made her feel as if she was part of a striptease.

She wanted to touch him like that, too. *She* wanted to lean against him, feel the warmth of his skin against her cheek, and inhale his masculine scent.

Celise had a small glimpse of him yesterday when he'd thrown off his shirt during the examination. He'd done that plenty of times before, but she'd never dared to take a good look.

But she looked now ...

It was impossible to tear her gaze away.

She wanted so badly to touch him, and shock rolled over her when Diane gave her an encouraging smile.

Calmness followed. She was finally *allowed* to touch the man she loved. Her whole body yearned for it.

Her hands reached for him as if in a trance. Celise stepped behind him, placing her fingers on his back, slowly guiding them around toward his hairless chest.

His muscles tensed when she made contact with his naked skin, and he inhaled deeply again. His skin was warm and soft over the fit muscles that made her fantasies go wild.

Wind groaned, and it filled her with hope as the temperature in her body rose. The bond didn't seem to be objecting.

She took her time, slowly getting used to the feel of

him. She could do this all day. She'd never grow tired of touching him.

Diane was watching her.

She looked away, and embarrassment flooded her, making her suddenly very aware of what she was doing, but the more time passed, the less she cared. Arousal made her burn like never before.

Celise wanted to take the next step and kiss him, but she didn't dare. She didn't want to risk hurting him again. Instead, she took a deep breath to gather courage and moved in front of Wind.

He remained still when she placed herself between his legs and wrapped her arms around him, closing her eyes. She inhaled his amazing scent, allowing it to soothe her senses like a perfect perfume would do.

Wind didn't hesitate and wrapped his arms around her, too.

Her heart clenched. Did he know it was her, or was he hoping she was Diane?

She opened her eyes when Diane tapped her arm. Reality slapped her in the face. This was not what they were supposed to be doing. She gave Diane a shy smile and moved away.

The understanding in Diane's eyes never went away. She moved in front of Wind and leaned closer, her lips almost touching his.

Wind reacted to her presence. A gentle grin played on his lips, and his curiosity was unmistakable.

Diane leaned even closer but stopped. She seemed to hesitate as if she was nervous. When she finally kissed him, she only pressed her lips against his for a short second, and then stepped back.

Surprise filled Celise, but then it hit her. Diane had tried to fool the bond into thinking *she* was her.

Celise swallowed, realizing it was her turn.

She placed herself between Wind's legs again, looking at his attractive face, but the growing fear refused to go away.

Would her kiss hurt him again? That was the last thing she wanted, but there was only one way to find out.

He seemed to get even more eager, as his grin widened. He searched for her hand.

She gave it to him, and he pulled her closer, wrapping his arms around her waist, giving her no other choice but to press her chest against his.

Her emotions went crazy from being this close to him. To feel his warm body and strong arms around her was like a drug. Without it, she longed for it, but with it, satisfaction followed, at least for a short while.

Celise tensed when he moved in for a kiss. He wasn't able to see her. She had to meet him halfway, but she hesitated again. In her mind, she relived him writhing in pain, but his inviting lips were too tempting to resist.

She took a deep breath and prepared for the worst as she pressed her lips to his. The softness of them ignited her undying fire, but she didn't dare to do more. Instead, she waited for the groan of pain she'd heard too many times by now, but seconds ticked by ... and nothing.

Wind opened his mouth and deepened the kiss. The heat between her legs intensified when his tongue touched hers. The kiss was slow, gentle, but passionate like never before. It made her tingle all over.

Her throat tightened, made it difficult to breathe, but Celise didn't mind. As long as he kept doing what he was doing, she'd be fine.

The haze his kiss pulled her into once again made her forget her shyness. Eagerness awakened within her instead. With each touch, with each gentle bite, or lick with his tongue, it became more and more difficult to stop.

She pressed herself so close to him as she possibly could, and he seemed just as unwilling to stop.

He pulled back and let out a deep groan that sent pleasure sweeping through her whole body.

Diane stood by Wind's side, and Celise didn't miss what she was doing. She touched him wherever she could reach, and when her hand moved to the inside of his thigh, he took a deep breath and shifted on the stole.

It made Celise look down. She gulped when she

noticed his pants were strained from the temptation they were hiding. The sight sent her into a new level of arousal, especially when Diane grazed his sex with slow and sensual caresses.

Wind let out a shaky breath and parted his legs more to make it easier to be touched. His eagerness was difficult to miss when he clenched and unclenched his hands.

Celise hadn't expected Diane to do that, especially not *in front* of her, and Wind's reaction didn't make it easier. Her sex clenched painfully, and her nipples hardened against the bra.

Before she was able to shake the surprise off, he was kissing her again. This time, the kiss was deeper, more intense, and filled with desire.

She couldn't hold back her moan. Her hands grabbed Wind's arms, gently squeezing his biceps to stop herself from jumping on his lap. It was becoming too much.

Wind's hands explored her body, making skin contact wherever he could touch without undressing her. He made her feel like he actually wanted her, as if it was *her* who was turning him on.

Without warning, Wind ripped off the blindfold. Passion was written all over his face. Desire shone strongly in his gaze. "I knew it was you. I felt no pain or discomfort." He kissed her again. He took control and demanded more, pushing his tongue into her mouth, and she felt him smile against her lips.

It filled her with joy.

Her happiness didn't last long.

Wind suddenly pushed her away as if she'd burnt him. He groaned and flew off the stool. He bent over, supporting himself against the bed frame.

Diane was instantly by his side. "Wind?" Worry was written all over her face.

He raised a hand. "Give me a minute." His voice sounded strained.

Neither Diane or Celise dared to move as he slowly recovered.

After a while, he exhaled audibly and straightened his back. Confusion sang in his eyes as he looked at Celise. "I don't understand. I *knew* I was kissing you. Your touch felt different from Diane's. I was turned on the way Diane's touch turns me on."

Disappointment filled Celise, but at the same time, she felt joy. It *had* worked, to a certain point.

"Do you want to try again? I'll kiss you first, and we'll see what will happen," Diane said.

Wind hesitated, but after a short moment, he took a deep breath and nodded. "All right." He sat on the stool and rewrapped the cloth around his head.

Diane moved closer and pressed her lips to his. The kiss was gentle and slow, filled with obvious sensual emotions that made Wind relax.

Celise tried to stay calm. The knowledge she'd caused him pain lingered in the back of her mind. They all had to go through this to save Wind, though. She had to forget it and move on. They had to try again ... no matter what.

The feeling of awkwardness slowly washed away. In the past, when she'd seen them holding hands or kiss, an intense ache had filled her heart. Now, when she watched them, she felt something completely different.

Arousal.

Wind's hands lay on Diane's hips as their tongues met in a kiss filled with love and devotion.

Celise could only imagine how difficult this had to be for them. She stared as the kiss grew deeper. She bit her lip; didn't want to remind them of what Jade had told them about touching each other like this.

Diane eventually pulled away, with a hazy gaze and flushed cheeks. "Your turn."

Celise swallowed and approached Wind.

His cheeks were flushed, too. His chest heaved as he breathed hard, and the arousal in his body was impossible to miss.

The shyness made her look away, but all she wanted was to touch him. There was so much of him to explore.

As he reached for her, his chest muscles worked. The appealing view made it almost impossible to keep her hands in check and not strip him in seconds.

He wrapped his strong arms around her and pulled her against him. A gentle but tense smile played on his full lips as he waited.

Celise slightly pulled away. "Wind ..."

His grip on her tightened. "Don't worry. I'll be all right shortly after if it doesn't work."

Celise nodded even if he couldn't see it. She said a silent pray and pressed her lips against his, hoping for the best.

The first few seconds were nerve-wracking, but when Wind didn't jerk away, hope awakened within her. Would it work this time?

He smiled against her lips as his arms pulled her closer. He wanted more, and she wanted to give him more, but if she deepened the kiss, things could turn bad again. Even if it was the last thing she wanted, she eventually pulled away.

Wind removed the cloth. "That went well."

"Kiss him now, without the blindfold," Diane said.

He tensed, and his smile faded. "Do it," he encouraged, but his expression only tightened even more.

Celise hesitated. She didn't like the apprehension in his eyes, but there was no other option. She braced herself and crushed her lips against Wind's. A second later, she jumped back and stared at him, waiting for his pain.

Wind groaned and leaned forward, remaining like that

for a while.

His pain filled her heart. She'd hurt him again. She hated it. She hated being the cause of his agony ... over and over again. "I'm so sorry, Wind."

He gave her a smile after righting himself. "It's not your fault, Celise. Don't ever think that. It's just my bond that's unwilling to let you in ... yet." He grabbed her arm and pulled her against him again, closing his arms around her. "But I can do this now."

The deep gaze he gave her awakened butterflies in her stomach.

He caressed her hair as if to comfort her. "I'm sure it's just a matter of time."

CHAPTER 12

Celise entered the bedroom with a pounding heart. Wind walked in after her and closed the door. The sound made her jump.

They were alone now.

"Did you enjoy dinner?" he asked as he came closer.

Celise turned around and looked at him. "Yes. Diane is a good cook."

He smiled. "Yes, she is. She enjoys cooking."

"Do you?"

Wind shrugged. "I don't mind it, but I can't say it's one of my favorite things to do."

Celise gazed at the bed. She couldn't help but notice that Wind was looking at it as well.

A gentle smile decorated his face, a smile that made her nerves grow.

It'd been a strange day. After the kissing game, they'd taken a break and had spent a few hours together, all three of them. They'd talked, laughed, and eaten as if nothing serious was going on. It had made them all relax, but night had finally fallen, and with it, the tension returned.

She'd brushed her teeth and taken care of her needs, and now, as she stood in front of him, the reality of what was about to happen sank in.

Her body trembled. She'd never touched him like that before. What they'd done earlier was nothing compared to what they would try to do now. "Do you really believe Diane is all right with this?"

"She is because she has to be."

Celise could only nod, but the feeling that she was intruding refused to go away.

"Should we try to get some sleep?"

She tensed. "Just sleep, right?"

Excitement flashed in his eyes, and Celise could swear Wind had changed since yesterday.

He'd gone from being completely uninterested in a relationship with her, to not having anything against her touch. Was he starting to feel things for her? Like now, when she looked into his marvelous, aluminum-colored, shining eyes, she couldn't help but wonder.

There was ... something.

"Is that all you want?" he asked.

96

Celise held her breath. "Um ... I don't know. I mean ... you're not ready yet ... are you?"

"We won't know unless we try."

She'd imagined many times what it'd be like to sleep with Wind, and now, the time had finally come. It felt surreal, and in her mind, Wind still belonged to Diane. Getting pass that was not easy.

He grabbed her shirt.

Celise jerked away. "What are you doing?"

"Undressing you."

"What for?"

He chuckled. "So that we can ... sleep."

Heat traveled to her cheeks. "Oh."

Wind moved closer, invading her personal space. "You're so nervous. Are you afraid of me?"

She shook her head and swallowed. "No, it's not that."

"Please, tell me."

His gentle voice was like the sweetest honey, caressing her chaotic emotions, calming her.

"Being this close to you—" Her words didn't come easy. "What happened today is more than I could've ever asked for."

He nodded. "Being finally touched by the one you love after so many years must be overwhelming."

She cleared her throat. "You can say that."

He studied her for a while without a word. He was

thinking. About what, she couldn't guess. "I have no idea how far we can take this, but let's try one step at a time, and see where we'll end up. If it doesn't work tonight, if my eyes won't flash, we can always try tomorrow or the day after that."

Celise blinked. "You're really willing to go through this, to make me your bound one, aren't you?"

"Yes. I thought it'd take longer for me to reach this point. I thought it'd take weeks to feel what I feel now, but my bond has been more co-operative than I expected. Maybe it's because we know each other, and maybe because I've kissed you on the cheek a few times in the past."

Celise inhaled deeply as hope awakened within her. "What does your bond tell you now, compared to yesterday?"

Wind hesitated. "It doesn't mind me touching you anymore. That's always something, but kissing you is obviously not okay yet." He lowered his gaze. "But I also feel like I'm not fair toward Diane. She's in another room, well aware of what we're about to do. It's tearing me apart that she has to go through this even if we all agreed to this."

Celise's heart clenched. "I understand." She looked down.

He put a finger under her chin, making her look at him. "You have the same look in your eyes you had yesterday when you thought I'm doing this only to survive." He cupped her cheeks. "Please, trust me. That's all I'm asking."

She swallowed. "I trust you, I really do, but it's hard when I know you'd rather be with Diane than me, and I don't blame you for it."

Hesitation lingered in his expression. "Something is pulling me to *you* now, Celise. Don't you see it? I enjoy looking at you and holding you in my arms."

She nodded, trying to see the positive in all this. "That sounds promising."

"It does." He nodded to the bed. "Shall we?"

Celise stared there again. Heat grew, making her lower parts clench. Her body burned for his touch, but the image of a sad Diane was hard to put aside.

Somehow, she had to.

She wanted Wind badly. He'd been her whole world for so many years. Excitement had filled her every time she'd seen him, making her long for the times when she'd been invited over to examine him. Only then could she touch him, and now, here she was, about to do so much more.

When he grabbed her shirt a second time and stripped it off, she didn't jerk away, but it made her more nervous than ever before. He draped the shirt on the stool.

Celise covered her breasts with her arms. She felt exposed even if most of her clothing was still on. At first, she didn't dare to look at Wind. She didn't want to see the lack of interest in his eyes. What if he didn't like her body? She was shorter than most women and didn't have a fit figure like Diane. Instead, she had a few pounds too much. Wasn't overweight, but it was enough to make her feel uncomfortable.

He gave a reassuring smile before he grabbed her arms and turned her around.

She gasped when his hands went for her bra. Feeling him open it sent a shiver through her. She couldn't help the squeak that fled her mouth as he tugged it off.

Wind wrapped his arms around her, pulling her against his chest. His hands traveled around her stomach and arms, feeling her.

The heat from his warm fingers against her naked skin was beyond amazing. "Shit," she said, unable to stop herself.

He chuckled. "I'm not going to eat you." He nipped at her earlobe, making her wince. "Well, maybe a little."

Celise closed her eyes and rested her head against his shoulder. She loved being touched by him like this. It almost made her forget all her worries.

She allowed herself to drown in everything he was willing to give.

"I actually like this," Wind said. "You have such soft and pale skin. My bond doesn't mind at all. Strange, huh? Who would've guessed it'd be this easy, this fast." His right hand went farther, toward the waistband of her black leggings. His fingertips slid in under them. "Do you want to find out if my bond will behave if I touch your pussy?"

She lost her capability to speak. She opened her mouth, but no words came out. Wanted to protest, to say she wasn't ready for that yet, but her body told another story. His words alone turned her on, and everything inside her screamed for more.

Wind's touch slowly moved under her pants when she didn't answer.

Celise was unable to stand still as he kept moving down slowly, torturous inch by torturous inch.

He was testing his bond.

His hand shook, and it didn't take much for her to realize he was nervous too, but nothing seemed *wrong*. His bond seemed to behave.

It was bliss. It was torture.

Especially when he finally reached his goal.

"This is fascinating." His voice shook. "I can touch you. I can actually *touch* you."

Celise smiled, glad his bond didn't object, but when his palm cupped her private area, she gasped. She arched her back against his chest when one of his fingers parted her and reached for her sensitive nub. "Oh my God," she squeaked.

He pressed his finger against her clit, circling with a

gentle pressure, making her body quiver harder. It was becoming difficult to stand.

She'd been with other men, but she'd never had a serious relationship. None of them had ever made her feel like this, either.

Wind's caress made her world spin, and her need for release was almost painful. If he'd stop, she'd scream.

"You're ready to fall apart in my arms," he whispered in her ear.

"Yes, please," she moaned and licked her lips. Celise wrapped her arms around his neck, leaving her completely exposed to him.

His other hand went for her breast as he added another finger and increased the pressure against her clit.

Celise closed her eyes and allowed her body to take over. Her need for him was so great there was no other way to go. She was lost in the pleasure.

She inhaled when Wind grabbed her nipple and pinched it, making it harden between his fingertips. She jolted and longed for more.

Everything around her faded. All there was was him. He placed gentle kisses on her neck. It made her shiver, awakening goosebumps on her skin.

His breathing seemed to become ragged along with hers. She felt his hot breath against her ear as he increased the pressure on her sensitive nerves. Wind went from being careful, to intense and determined. He knew what he was doing, and when she couldn't handle more, her body ignited.

Celise's knees gave out beneath her as she came, but Wind didn't allow her to fall as he worked her mercilessly. She was unable to hold back her scream.

Wind made her feel so good, and he'd made her come so hard it was impossible to hold back.

When it was over, she collapsed in his arms. A thin coat of sweat had broken out on her skin. There was no strength left in her, but she'd never been happier.

He lifted her up in his arms and carried her to the bed. He laid her on the sheets and gave her a gentle smile, but she didn't miss the sad look in his eyes.

"Are you all right?" she asked.

He nodded. "Yes, I'm fine. Don't worry." He grabbed his shirt and tugged it off.

He had satisfied her, but the sight of his bare skin stirred her desire again. His broad shoulders, muscular chest, and perfect fair complexion made her realize she hadn't had the chance to really touch him yet, to explore his body.

She met his gaze, studying him. He'd always made her feel like she could turn to him, no matter what. He'd always cherished their friendship, despite her feelings for him. Wind had never turned his back on her, and she'd never seen him angry.

These last two days were the first time she'd seen him frustrated, but it was understandable. He was losing his bound one and was forced to bind himself to another woman to survive.

Celise sat up and grabbed his hand, making him sit on the bed. "I'm so sorry, Wind for all you have to go through. I've always had your support, and I promise, you'll always have mine. No matter what happens, you can always turn to me. I'll always be there for you."

He blinked and surprise crossed his face.

"I mean it," she went on. "I'll be the bound one you deserve to have."

Wind smiled then. "Thank you, Celise. I believe you. I know how strong your love for me is. Even if I wasn't sure at first, I do believe now that you're the one for me. Only you can replace Diane. No one else."

His words warmed her heart, but they made it ache, as well. She was still a replacement, but she couldn't focus on that. She blinked away tears. "You don't want me to—?"

He hesitated. "I'm not there yet. I enjoyed touching you, but—"

Celise's heart fell to her stomach. "I understand." Her cheeks burned from embarrassment, hurt radiated.

"Don't be ashamed, Celise. It's not your fault." He squeezed her hand. "We've come further than I ever dared to imagine in just one day. If it continues like this, my eyes will flash soon." He looked at her lips. "I want to kiss you."

She winced. "Why?"

Amusement filled his eyes. "Because I feel like it. I'll pull back if the bond protest."

Celise prepared herself for the worst as Wind leaned closer.

He stopped just inches from her face. He tensed and seemed to be preparing himself as well. Then he pressed his lips against hers for two seconds and pulled away.

Their gazes met.

"Well?" she asked.

"I didn't feel any objection from the bond."

She smiled. "Try again."

Wind didn't hesitate this time. He perched over her on all four and pressed his mouth to hers.

She loved the feeling of his warm and gentle lips. If she hadn't known he wasn't in love with her, the kiss would've fooled her.

Butterflies danced in Celise's stomach. For the first time ever, she got to experience what it was like to lie beneath him. He wasn't directly on top of her, but close enough. It became almost impossible to resist the impulse to wrap her arms around him.

His eyes were closed, and Wind rested his hand against her cheek, kissing her slowly without pushing his tongue inside her mouth, but it was enough to get her worked up again. Especially since he seemed to be enjoying himself.

But then Wind jerked away with a groan. He pushed off the bed and grimaced. "Fuck, that hurt."

Celise flew up, ready to comfort him, but he raised his hand.

"Give me a moment."

His words hurt. Not because they made her feel rejected, but because the kiss hadn't worked.

Almost a minute passed before he finally relaxed. "I'm all right now."

"I don't understand why this is happening. You should be able to kiss me if you can touch me."

Wind remained silent for a few seconds. "I think the bond finds the kissing too intimate. It has accepted that I touch you, but it seems like kissing is a completely different thing."

Celise blinked. "That sounds strange."

He undressed but left his underwear on.

The sight of him made her almost speechless. She could do nothing but stare. He usually had loose pants on, hiding his long legs, but now, when she was able to *see* them, she was amazed by how muscular they were.

"Let's go to sleep." He encouraged her with a smile.

Her shyness returned as she took off her clothes too. It didn't matter if he'd had his hands on her or seen her upper body naked. Letting him see the rest of her made her hot all over, even if she'd kept her panties on.

Celise hurried under the linens. It only made Wind chuckle.

He lay behind Celise, spooning her. His body heat instantly surrounded her, and she was in heaven.

She could stay like this forever. It was a dream come true, and the best part was that he didn't seem to mind being here with her.

Wind held her tightly pressed against his body. "Are you comfortable?"

"Yes," she said with a lazy voice. "Are you?"

"Yes, very much so. Sleep now. I'm not going anywhere."

She closed her eyes and smiled to herself. Sleep slowly swept over her as exhaustion encouraged her to rest. The silence in the room and Wind's body heat made her drowsy. She felt safe, she even felt loved and cared for. A feeling she hadn't felt for a long, long time, but as she slipped into the world of dreams, Celise could've sworn she'd heard a silent cry coming from afar.

CHAPTER 13

Celise opened her eyes and yawned. She'd slept like a baby. No wonder considering what she'd been through the past day.

It was far from over, but at this very moment, she was happy. She lay on a comfortable bed, covered with white linens, and was surrounded by a pleasant warmth.

The sun was shining outside, spreading a bright light inside the room.

Wind lay beside her, still asleep.

She couldn't help but smile and admire his handsome face.

Wind breathed slowly. He looked relaxed, and she didn't miss the gentle smile on his lips. Was he dreaming about something nice?

A lock of his brown hair lay over his forehead. Celise

brushed it away and touched his warm skin. It made her heart jump. She wanted nothing more but to move closer and embrace him, but she pulled her hand back instead. She didn't want to wake him. He needed his sleep, too.

The best part was that Wind really was trying to transfer his bond to her even if it caused him great pain. That meant a lot to her, because his love for Diane was strong, and that would never change.

She hated being the one to take him away. She wanted Diane and Wind to be happy. She wanted her to live, even if it meant she'd never be with him. He preferred Diane, and always would. They were so much more alike.

Celise sighed. This was a complicated situation that gave her a headache. She didn't want to hurt Diane, but hurt was unavoidable, probably for all three of them.

She remembered the crying she'd heard before falling asleep. At first, she'd thought she'd imagined it, that her fatigue had played tricks on her, but now she knew it had been Diane. Without a doubt.

Celise knew what she had to do. It didn't matter how much she wanted to stay in bed with Wind, she and Diane needed to talk. They still hadn't had the chance just the two of them.

She glanced at Wind one final time. He was still asleep and didn't wake when she climbed out of bed.

Celise put her clothes on and left the room. She headed

for the bathroom, took care of her needs, brushed her teeth, and combed her hair. When she was ready, she went looking for Diane. Hopefully, she was awake.

She headed for the room Diane had taken last night and knocked on the door. At first, there was only silence.

"Come in," Diane finally said.

With a heavy heart, Celise entered the room. It wasn't big. It had a rectangular shape, with space for a bed and a wardrobe. The interior was bright and appealing, just like the rest of the house. It was a guestroom, and it made her heart clench even more.

Her friend had spent the night alone in her own guestroom.

On the other end of the room were wide open doors leading to a balcony with white metal railings. Diane sat out there on an armchair with her back to Celise.

She swallowed and stepped out on the balcony.

It was warm, but Diane's legs were covered with a blanket. A small, round table stood by the chair. A hot cup of tea with a tiny slice of lemon in it rested there. Steam rose from the cup.

Celise studied Diane. She didn't look well at all, with the dark bags under her eyes and uncombed hair. Her skin was paler than usual, and her hands and lips had a bluish hue. She seemed to be freezing.

Maybe their activities last night with Wind had been

too much for her.

"Good morning, Celise." Diane smiled.

Celise swallowed hard. "Good morning."

"Did you and Wind bond?"

Heat rushed to Celise's cheeks as she leaned against the railings. "Not yet."

Concern crossed her friend's expression. "You weren't able to have sex?"

Unease swept over Celise. Telling Diane these things didn't feel right. She was his bound one after all. "He could touch me, but ... um ... couldn't kiss me for long, and he wasn't able to—" Celise looked away.

"I see." Diane was quiet for a while before she sighed. "I guess we still have things to work on then."

"Jade said this could take time, but I believe we've accomplished a lot for one day."

"Yes, I agree. He knows you and likes you. That's probably why."

Another silence filled the balcony.

"Diane, I—" Celise lost her words.

Diane's lips twitched. "I know what you're going to say."

She winced. "You do?"

"You feel like you're stealing Wind from me. Am I right?"

Celise held her breath as she nodded.

"I chose this. I proposed this to Wind, and he accepted.

You don't have to feel like that, because I'm glad you're the one to take over the bond. You're the best option." Diane grabbed her arm. "I'm calmer knowing he'll be safe with you once I'm gone. Seeing him with a stranger would've given me a stomach ache." She smiled. "I'm glad you chose him, too."

Celise stared at Diane. She had no idea what she should say.

"I'm all right with this. I really am, Celise."

"But ... I heard you cry."

Her friend's smile faded. "Well, those things are unavoidable. He means the world to me, and when I heard you last night—" Her gaze turned serious. "Don't get me wrong. I love Wind with all my heart, but I'll also do everything in my power to make sure the bond is transferred to you. The last thing I want is him dying with me, or worse, ending up as one of the Fighters."

Celise agreed. "I don't want that either."

"After listening to what Shade and Phoebe had to say about Nightmare and his gang, I can't stand the thought of my gentle Wind being among them. If my death doesn't kill him, they would. One way or another."

She shivered. She'd heard Shade's and Phoebe's story as well, and it hadn't been pretty.

Nightmare had injured Shade by trying to remove his bond to Phoebe. He'd tried to replace it with another signal, to make Shade forget her. The rogue leader had been sure it'd work, but it hadn't. Shade had almost died. He'd spent days in MedAct's care after that. Now, Phoebe's cyborg was in her care. She checked him every other day and reported back to Jade. So far, things seemed all right.

"So, what do we do today?" Celise asked.

"I guess we continue where we ended yesterday. Wind can touch you now, but he can't kiss you. We must make sure you two have sex as soon as possible."

They'd always seemed so open about sex, but Celise had a hard time with that. "Do you think you'll need to—?" The words died in her mouth.

A grin appeared on Diane's lips. "I don't know. Maybe. Is that something you'd mind?"

"I .. um ... I don't know ..."

Diane studied her. "Have you ever slept with a man? You seem so shy about sex and intimacy."

"Yes, I have. I've had a few relationships, but my work has always been more important to me."

"So you don't have much experience?"

She shook her head.

"Well, I guess it's a good thing Wind and I have plenty of experience."

Celise almost jerked out of her skin. "What?"

Diane chuckled. "Don't look so surprised. He and I have experimented a lot over the years. We both have high sex drives, and once the bond is yours, you'll have all that to yourself. I'm sure Wind will want to teach you all about it."

Celise couldn't stop staring at Diane as all kinds of images crossed her mind of Wind in different sexual positions. She'd never believed Wind was into sex that much. He didn't seem the type.

"I don't mind a threesome, just so you know, Celise. If that's what has to happen then don't be afraid to ask me. I'm sure Wind won't mind either."

Celise was unable to answer. Her jaw dropped, and the back of her neck went hot, searing into her cheeks.

"I shocked you, didn't I?"

She closed her mouth and tried not to imagine all three of them in bed, but strangely enough, a tiny hint of interest awakened within her.

"I know I did," Diane went on with an undying smile.

The door to the room opened, and Celise winced.

Wind entered the room and joined them. He was dressed in black sweatpants and a white shirt. His hair was wet, and his skin almost seemed to glow from freshness.

It made her heart stutter. He was breathtaking with his fit and elegant features, and he looked her right in the eyes. He didn't seem the slightest ashamed of what they'd done before going to sleep. She, on the other hand, couldn't escape the embarrassment flushing her.

"Good morning, ladies." He approached Diane, bent down, and kissed her on the cheek.

Diane caressed his arm. "Good morning, love."

When he straightened and turned to her, Celise tensed. He approached her slowly, looking her deep into the eyes. Excitement lingered in his. "Celise." His voice was like the sweetest whisper, teasing her tingling insides.

She swallowed and nodded, unable to say his name.

He cupped her face and gave her a look that made her melt on the inside.

Celise didn't move. She *couldn't* move. His touch almost made her forget to breathe. His masculine and appealing scent hit her senses. He smelled fresh from his shower, like an ocean breeze.

He bent down to kiss her but stopped before his lips touched hers. Wind tilted her head to the side and went for her throat instead.

Celise was unable to hold back a gasp as his lips made contact with her sensitive skin. He made her shiver all over. She closed her eyes as warmth in her body rose, making her head spin.

He nibbled her earlobe as his hands explored her form.

She loved it. She hated it. Diane was watching, and that made it awkward.

Wind pulled back with a wide smile. "The bond wouldn't let me kiss your lips, but kissing you elsewhere is apparently acceptable."

"Good." She tried to shake off the arousal, but it was an impossible task. He aroused her just by being close to her, and when he touched her, she drowned in her own fire. Celise didn't miss the grin on Diane's lips.

"I must say it's rather arousing watching you two," her friend said.

Anticipation filled Wind's shiny gaze, and when Celise saw pride in them as well, it hit her. He'd do *anything* to please Diane.

"You liked it? Do you want me to kiss her again?" he asked.

Celise held her breath. He definitely wanted to please Diane. Would he want to please her too once she was his bound one?

Diane chuckled. "I think Celise has had enough for now. She looks ready to fall apart."

He gave her a once-over. "She's aroused." Wind glanced back at Diane, his gaze lingering on the bed inside the guestroom. "I could take care of her need if you want me to. My bond allows me to do that now."

Shock rippled through Celise. They discussed her and sex so … casually.

Wind noticed. "Don't worry. I won't hurt you. I can ease your need the way I did last night. I'm sure you're going to like it."

116

Celise couldn't avoid a look toward the bed. "In here?"

"Yes."

"With Diane here?"

"Is that a problem?"

She couldn't believe what she was hearing. "You really don't mind her seeing us together, do you?"

He frowned. "Should I? She's still my bound one, and Diane doesn't mind us being together. So if she doesn't mind, then I'm fine with it, too."

Celise sighed. "If Diane wasn't … dying, would you agree to it as well?"

He winced. "Of course not! Only my bound one touches me, and I only touch my bound one. I'm touching you because you're becoming my new bound one."

Celise nodded and relaxed.

Diane rose from the armchair and wrapped the blanket around her shoulders. "You've nothing to worry about, Celise. If it turns out I have to be with you and Wind, I'll treat it professionally."

Celise swallowed hard. "I understand, but I never thought we'd have to go that far."

"Who knows. Maybe we won't."

Something rang from the bedroom. Wind went inside and approached a small and flat screen attached to the wall. He pressed its right corner, and the signal stopped. Phoebe's attractive face appeared on the screen.

"Hello, Phoebe," he said with a smile.

"Hi, Wind. You don't happen to know where Celise is, do you? I've tried to call her, but she isn't answering."

"She's right here."

Celise approached the screen. "I'm sorry you had to search for me, I've been here since yesterday."

Surprise crossed Phoebe's eyes before she glanced at Wind. "Is something wrong with you?" She gasped and placed a hand against her mouth. "Is Diane all right?"

"Don't worry," Wind said. "We're both fine."

Phoebe studied them. Obviously, she wasn't convinced. "Very well," she said after a moment. "We had an appointment today, Celise."

Celise gasped. "I completely forgot."

Her friend grinned. "I figured."

"Give me a few minutes, and I'll be there."

Phoebe nodded. "See you soon." She hung up.

Wind turned to her. "I'm going with you." There was unexpected anger in his eyes.

She studied him. "Maybe you should stay with Diane."

Diane entered the room. "It's better if he goes with you. He's supposed to be by your side from now on, not mine."

He nodded. "No way I'm staying here when Shade will be near you."

Celise's jaw dropped.

Where had that come from all of a sudden?

CHAPTER 14

Diane watched them drive away from the balcony. She followed the disappearing car until she couldn't see them anymore.

Joy and sadness mixed inside her heart.

She knew why Wind had been so eager to go with Celise. His protective instincts had awakened, and he didn't want another cyborg near her.

It meant the transfer was working.

He was becoming Celise's.

Maybe she wasn't aware of it yet, but Diane didn't doubt Wind would make her see it soon enough. A cyborg always felt overprotective of his bound one. It also meant he'd be safe once she was gone. It was a worry Diane had had ever since she'd found out she was sick.

Diane swallowed down tears. She had to stay strong. This was for the best. She was doing this for Wind. He had to live.

Diane took a deep breath, closed her eyes, and allowed a feeling of calmness fill her. Even if things were difficult, they were heading in the right direction, and Wind was so brave.

It was impossible to miss his pain, and that he didn't want to do this. It had been so obvious yesterday, but today, it seemed easier for him. Diane was grateful for that.

A wave of pain hit her in the chest, making her moan and lean forward. Sweat broke out on her skin, and her body started to tremble. She sat still and tried to breathe through it. One minute passed, two more followed before the agony finally faded.

Diane exhaled and reclined in the chair, exhausted. She always felt so weak afterward, but she'd gotten used to this over the past year. Inflammation had broken out in her body, slowly killing her. Fever was a regular thing for her now. Luckily, today seemed to be a feverless day.

Diane didn't know how long she sat like that, but she was glad Wind wasn't there to see. She didn't want him to see her at her weakest. She wanted him to remember her as she used to be, happy and full of energy.

A memory crossed her mind.

They'd been in Wind's study, painting on canvases. Or at least, they'd been trying to. Before long, they'd started painting each other instead. It had ended with him taking her on the floor, both covered in paint.

Diane smiled.

She hoped Wind would create such memories with Celise. She prayed he'd be happy with her.

She liked the amazing and intelligent woman, even if Celise was rather shy, but Diane didn't doubt Wind would make her relax and open up more. Once she got used to him, it shouldn't be an issue. At least, Diane hoped for that.

The transfer was being made at the last minute.

Diane doubted she had many more months left. Her health had decreased rapidly the last two weeks, and that worried her, but she tried not to think about it. She'd wanted to wait and see if she'd improve, and that had been foolish of her.

Now, all she could do was hope the bond would be in Celise's hands before she took her last breath.

Diane reached beneath the armchair and pulled out a thick photo album. She opened it, and browsed slowly, looking at each image for a few seconds.

The book was filled with photos of her and Wind. In the beginning, there were images of their time at MedAct, his first month as a newborn. The doctor, Alexander Fleming, who'd created Wind was in several of the images. He'd been in his early thirties back then, and he'd also been the owner of MedAct before Jade Silva.

Wind had been so innocent back then. The calmness he'd radiated had filled her with peace. He'd been just what she'd needed after living a stressful and hectic life for thirty years.

Her cyborg had brought her back to the present and given her a purpose. She'd created him to never feel lonely again, after being abandoned by both her parents and ex-husband.

It had been the best decision of her life.

When Celise had come into their lives a few years ago, Diane had instantly seen her fascination in Wind. It had bothered her at first, but as time had passed by, she'd realized Celise was harmless, and that her love for Wind was pure.

The girl had never tried to take Wind away from her, and today, Diane was thankful for Celise.

Diane remembered Alexander as a gentle soul with kind eyes and a huge passion for his work. It had been amazing to work with him. He'd always been supportive and had answered any questions she'd had. He'd always made her feel safe, and when Wind had opened his eyes, she'd known the right doctor had created him.

When she remembered what had happened to Alexander, a string of sorrow washed over her.

She and Alexander had stayed in contact after she

and Wind had gone home. They'd been supervised by him during the first two years of Wind's life, and he'd also become a close friend, but during those two years, Alexander had changed. He'd gone from being joyful to always looking over his shoulder.

Diane had no idea what'd happened to him, but something had taken away his smile. He'd even stopped spending time with them, but she still remembered their last conversation.

"Are you happy, Diane?" Alexander asked. "Is Wind everything you dreamt of?"

Diane nodded. "He is. I'm so happy to have him in my life. I don't know where I'd be without him." She moved away from the front door. "Do you want to come inside for a cup of tea?"

He seemed restless. He licked his lips and wrung his hands as he shook his head. "Thank you, but I just came by to make sure everything is all right." The doctor paused. "The bond, is it still functioning as it should?"

She blinked. "Of course. You checked it just a few weeks ago. Don't you remember?"

He seemed taken aback, as if he'd forgotten. "Yes, yes, I remember."

Diane studied him. "Are you all right? You seem stressed."

"I'm just having a tough day." Alexander peaked inside

the hallway without moving away from the door. "Is Wind here?"

"He's upstairs, painting. We're preparing for a new exhibition in a few months. Our paintings are in high demand. We almost have to work around the clock." She smiled, but her worry for Alexander didn't go away.

He nodded, rubbing his hands against each other again. "That's good. It sounds like you're both safe."

Diane frowned. "Shouldn't we be?"

Alexander didn't answer. Instead, he whirled toward his car. "I have to go. Take good care of him, Diane."

She winced. "What is—?"

The doctor raised his hand to interrupt her. "Just take good care of him. And Diane ... remember ..." He stopped and looked her deep into the eyes. "Wind has a choice."

She opened her mouth to ask what he'd meant, but Alexander hurried away. He got into his car, and before she even had the chance to grasp what'd just happened, he drove away.

Two days later, Alexander was gone.

He'd vanished. Just like that.

His car had been found abandoned along the highway in the middle of the night, but with no trace of the doctor.

Even now, no one knew what'd happened to him.

Diane browsed through the photo album again. She

stopped on a picture of him.

A tall and well-built man looked up at her from the photo that'd been taken at his office the day she and Wind had left MedAct. She and Wind stood next to him. Happiness beamed from both of them. It'd been a really wonderful day.

Alexander's shaggy black hair was combed backward. Strands of gray decorated his head and short beard despite his youth. He wore his white doctor coat and a wide smile on his face. He looked proud, and she knew he'd been that day.

Wind had been one of his finest cyborgs. Alexander had admitted that to her.

Diane closed the photo album and rested her head against the backrest. She closed her eyes. Fatigue swept through her once more. "Where ever you are, my friend, I hope you're happy."

CHAPTER 15

Wind got out of Celise's car and looked at Shade's and Phoebe's big villa. It was a beautiful white one-story house with an appealing garden without too much vegetation. He'd always enjoyed coming here, but this time it was different.

Looking at the house didn't make him want to go near it, and no way in hell he'd allow Celise to come here alone. Not anymore, at least. From now on, he'd always be with her.

There was another cyborg in there, and he didn't like it. He knew Shade, and Shade was bound to Phoebe, but it didn't matter. The thought of Shade being alone with Celise during his examination rubbed Wind the wrong way.

"Are you all right?" she asked.

"I'm fine." His words left his mouth a little too fast, and

he instantly regretted his harsh tone when Celise winced.

"Have I done something wrong?"

He frowned. "No, of course not. Why do you think that?"

"You seem so uptight since Phoebe called."

Wind took her hands in his. "I promise, I'm fine. A lot of things are going on right now. That's all."

Her expression softened. "I understand." Celise locked the car, and they approached the front door.

He couldn't help but tense when Celise knocked.

Someone approached the door from the inside, and he tightened his grip on her hand.

He wasn't hurting her, but surprise crossed her face when he pulled her against him.

A smiling Faye opened the door. Her long, blonde hair hung down her shoulders as curiosity lingered in her eyes as she looked them over.

"Faye?" Celise asked.

"Yep. Surprised to see me?" She grinned. "I thought I'd come by since it's the last day before Shade and Phoebe go on their vacation." Faye looked around. "Isn't Diane with you?"

"No, she isn't feeling the best today. She decided to stay at home."

Faye made a fake-sounding gasp. "But Wind, how dare you leave your bound one behind? That's not very thoughtful of you, especially when she isn't feeling well."

He'd never had any issues with Faye, but she could be a handful, and teasing him right now was not a good idea. "It's a long story."

Her grin darkened. "I'm sure it is."

He didn't answer, but his suspicion grew. Did Faye know?

They had to tell everyone eventually, but he couldn't be the one to say it. Everything inside him still protested, even if his bond had started to accept Celise. *She* had to be the one to tell everyone.

It would be less painful that way, physically.

The tension he'd felt since Phoebe called only grew as they entered the house.

Shade stood with his bound one in the hallway, greeting them with wide smiles.

Wind tried to smile back, but it came out stiff. He pulled Celise even closer, just in case. The thought of the other cyborg touching her made his stomach turn.

Shade's smile faded and his gaze narrowed as he studied them.

"We can't stay long," Celise said. "We must return to Diane soon."

Phoebe studied them, too. "Why in such a hurry? I thought we could drink tea after the exam, and talk a little."

Faye crossed her arms and grinned. "It's a long story."

Phoebe arched an eyebrow. "What do you mean?"

Faye shrugged. "It's not my story to tell."

Wind nodded to himself. Faye did indeed know. Celise had probably told her. It didn't bother him. It was no secret, but he still preferred his new bound one shared the news.

He had more important things to focus on, like keeping a watchful eye on Shade.

What if the cyborg all of a sudden touched Celise?

"What story?" Shade asked, and took a step closer.

Wind saw red, and slid in front of Celise, blocking the cyborg's way to her.

A loud gasp went through the hallway.

Shade halted in the middle of a step. He stared at Wind with huge eyes and an open mouth.

Wind glared at him and bared his teeth, daring him to come closer. Shade probably just wanted to stand nearer as they spoke, he meant no harm, but Wind's mind didn't care. The cyborg was close enough as it was.

Faye laughed. "This is getting better and better."

"What the hell's going on?" Phoebe yelled. "Wind, what's gotten into you? Why are you threatening Shade? You're acting like a newborn cyborg all of a sudden!"

He winced and focused on Phoebe. "Newborn?"

"Yes! You look ready to attack Shade just the way a

newborn would when he wants to defend his bound one. Don't you remember how it was?" She grabbed Shade's arm and tried to pull him back, but he wouldn't budge.

Shade looked ready to defend himself. His glass-like eyes shone with an intense glow. His big muscles were tense and his hands fisted. His mouth was a straight line, and his gaze set on Wind.

The atmosphere in the house was filled with insecurity.

From the corner of his eye, Wind noticed worry in the women's eyes, but he was unable to stop himself. He glared at Shade. Phoebe kept talking, but he was deaf to her words. His focus was on the other cyborg. The threat that could hurt his Celise.

If Shade dared to make just one move ...

He wasn't small, but not as large as Shade. It didn't matter. Wind wouldn't allow that to stop him. Taking Shade down wouldn't be easy, but if it came down to it, he'd protect Celise.

No matter what.

"Wind!"

He jerked when Faye shouted his name.

"Snap out if it, damn it!" she yelled, anger radiating from her eyes.

Wind blinked. Realization hit him, and he gasped. He'd been seconds away from attacking Shade. He shook his head to try to clear his thoughts. "I'm sorry. I never expected to react like this." He tried to relax, but the need to protect Celise from Shade was overwhelming. The cyborg still stood too close.

"What are you talking about?" Phoebe asked.

Wind took a deep breath. He had to be the one to say it, after all. Hopefully, it wouldn't be too painful. "I'm transferring my bond to Celise. On paper, she's already my bound one. It's a process that'll take some time. We've achieved more than expected in one day, but there's still a long way to go." He waited for the pain, but to his surprise, it never came.

Phoebe and Shade stared at him with wide eyes and dropped jaws.

Faye's laughter filled the room. "I told you it's quite a story."

Wind looked at Celise. She seemed unsure of what to do, and he didn't blame her. His unexpected reaction must've surprised her, too. He wrapped his arm around her waist in an attempt to comfort her.

She met his gaze, tense and confused, but when he slid his hand down her back, she relaxed, and a smile appeared in the corner of her lips.

He smiled back. Everything was all right.

Wind glanced toward Shade and Phoebe again.

They still stared at him.

"That means Diane—" Phoebe closed her mouth.

He nodded. "Diane's dying. We don't know how long she has, but not long. If she dies before my bond's transferred to Celise, I'll die with her, and that's the last thing Diane wants." Wind stood still, trying not to show the emotional chaos that went on inside him. The thought of losing Diane was unbearable.

Phoebe took a deep breath. "I understand." She let go of Shade. "That means you're in transition right now. That would explain your sudden need to protect Celise. The bond's new to you, just like it's new to a newborn cyborg." She went silent for a moment. "You do understand Celise has to touch Shade to examine him, right?"

Wind clenched his fists. "I know."

"Is it wise of you to be here, then?"

He pulled Celise even closer. "I'm not leaving Celise."

Phoebe sighed. "Since I know how strong the protective instincts are for you guys when you're newborn, I doubt they're any different for you now. That means there's no way in hell I'm letting you stay here and watch Celise examine Shade. It has to be done before we go on our trip, and I won't allow you to get in our way."

Wind glared at Phoebe. "I'm not leaving."

She threw out with her arms. "Wind, it's *us*! Do you really believe any of us will hurt Celise?"

He hesitated. "No, but it doesn't matter. I'll snap if Shade touches her."

Phoebe gave a frustrated sigh. "And that's why you can't be here."

"Let's tie Shade down," Faye said.

Everyone stared in her direction.

"What?" She shrugged. "I'm not suggesting some kinky game. What's wrong with you people?" She flashed a wicked grin before becoming serious. "If Shade's tied, Wind will have no reason to attack him as Celise examines him."

Phoebe shook her head. "You've got to be kidding me."

Shade stood silently, with an unpleased expression. Faye's idea seemed to appeal to him as little as it appealed to Phoebe.

"I think it actually might work," Celise said.

Phoebe shot her an irritated glare. "What?"

"Let me explain. We don't have to go as far as to tie Shade. It should be enough if we blind him. We all know how strong a cyborg's need to protect their bound one is, especially from another cyborg. It's not something they have much control over. You know that yourself, Phoebe. And if that's what Wind's feeling right now, we should listen. Forbidding him to be here will only make it worse, but stopping Shade from *seeing* me will make him immobile, and that might calm Wind's bond."

Wind smiled. "I think that's a good idea."

Shade looked unhappy but sighed. "Let's try it. We have no time to lose, and they have to get back to Diane. The last thing we want is Wind still being bound to her if she dies."

He gave Shade a grateful look.

Phoebe nodded. "Fine. Let's go into the living room. It's big enough to move around in if Wind snaps." She looked at Shade. "I'm staying with you." He opened his mouth to say something, but Phoebe raised her hand. "Don't argue with me. It'll be a pointless discussion." She turned to Faye. "You can wait in the kitchen."

Faye gasped, and her eyes widened. "No way! If Wind loses it, I want to be where the drama is. Besides, I doubt Shade's the shy type. I'm sure he won't mind showing some skin, right Shade?" She grinned.

Shade growled. "I told you before. You'll never touch me. I'm bound to Phoebe."

She snorted and rolled her eyes. "And *I* told you I know that." She headed into the living room.

"I swear, I'll strangle that woman one day," Shade muttered so quietly that Phoebe and Celise wouldn't be able to hear, but Wind caught it, and couldn't help his smile. He understood Shade's frustration so well.

Wind looked at Celise and felt the shift inside him as his bond accepted her a little bit more. That she'd chosen to listen to him meant a lot. It was almost as if each time she showed him understanding and patience, the bond let her in another inch.

And maybe, there was a tiny hint of ... love.

CHAPTER 16

Celise put her bag on the wooden table in Phoebe's and Shade's living room. She opened it and pulled out a scanning device she was well familiar with. She used it to examine all cyborgs in Glaswell.

The small machine was frequently used by all MedAct's medical staff as well. With one simple scan, it could say exactly what was wrong, and what had to be done. It saved a lot of time. She could then send the information to MedAct through the device. That saved a lot of time, too.

Celise loved her job. Getting the chance to work with cyborgs and get to know more about them made her life worth living. She was one of MedAct's Medical Advisers. It meant she had a medical education, but she wasn't allowed to create cyborgs. At least not yet. She still had a few more years of fieldwork before she could apply for that education, but she couldn't wait until the day. One of her goals was to find out why there were no female cyborgs. Barely anything was written about them in all the books she'd read. All she knew today was that the female cyborg program didn't work.

Wind stopped beside her and watched her.

She gave him a shy smile. Looking at him always awakened that reaction within her, but this time, she felt happiness instead of longing.

Somehow the transfer of the bond was working. His sudden possessive behavior was a turning point, but it didn't stop her from worrying. Celise had never worked with newborn cyborgs, but she was familiar with their possessiveness when it came to their bound one.

She'd read about it, and she'd spoken with many cyborgs, and each and everyone told her the same thing — it was almost impossible to control at first. Some had snapped as soon as a male approached their bound one, and didn't matter if it was a human male or a cyborg male.

Celise studied Wind. Would he snap too if she put her hands on Shade?

The anger and determination in his eyes was unusual. The calm and gentle Wind was still under the surface, but this was a side of him she'd never seen before.

In the end, the examination had to be completed, didn't matter what Wind thought. This was her job. She took care of many other cyborgs under doctor Jade Silva's supervision. Wind would have to get used to it. He already knew what she did. After all, she'd examined him for years.

She glanced at her friends. Faye sat on the couch. Phoebe stood next to it with crossed arms and worry in her eyes. Shade looked tense.

"Shade, this has to be your decision," Celise told him.

He nodded. "Let's just do this."

She nodded too and swallowed. Anything could happen now. Her hands shook as she activated the scanner. "You know the procedure."

The tension in his shining eyes became even more obvious.

Celise didn't doubt that Shade wasn't fond of the unwanted audience, but he didn't have a choice but to strip in front of everyone.

Phoebe's cyborg threw off his shirt and wrapped it around his eyes. "Do it." His voice was cold.

She couldn't help but notice Shade's naked and hairless torso or how his rippled muscles worked under smooth skin. He had a body that would make any woman want to touch him, but she felt no such desire. He was beautiful, but her heart beat for someone else.

Celise glanced at Wind again.

He looked even angrier than before. His hands were clenched into fists. His gaze was dark and set on Shade. His chest sank and rose fast as if he was breathing hard. It looked like he was fighting with himself. Everything in his posture said he was ready to attack.

Guilt filled her. She shouldn't have looked at Shade. "Wind?" Celise could barely control her shaky voice.

"I'm good," Wind said between clenched teeth.

The scanner almost fell from her hand when she approached Shade. She had to do this fast. Wind was ready to snap.

Shade didn't move, but it was obvious he didn't enjoy standing half-naked in front of everybody with his t-shirt wrapped around his head, especially since he couldn't easily defend himself if he needed to. Any other day, she would have giggled from how funny he looked, but the tension in the room prevented her from it.

Celise pushed a few buttons on the scanner, programming it to read Shade's data. It would scan his entire body, and make sure the cybernetics functioned as they should.

Shade's bond to Phoebe was damaged. That was why she was here, ordered by Doctor Jade Silva to keep an extra eye on him.

Shade was bound to Phoebe the way a cyborg should be, but every scanning she'd done since he'd left MedAct showed permanent damage. The bond would never be the same again, but thankfully, the harm wasn't extensive.

"I'm ready to begin," Celise said.

She placed the device against Shade's naked chest.

He took a deep breath when its cold surface touched his skin.

The scanner started reading him. Celise watched the small screen where information about Shade showed up. It was everything from his blood levels to how his cybernetics functioned. He seemed fine, but when it scanned the bond, a warning came up.

She read it, but like before, there was nothing to worry about. It was the same warning as always. All she could do was confirm that the warning had been received and allow the device to continue scanning Shade.

Silence lingered in the room.

She looked around. Everyone stared at her.

Faye seemed rather curious, worry shone in Phoebe's eyes, but anger flickered in Wind's shining, metallic eyes.

How she loved those eyes, even if they were filled with rage right now. She gave him a smile and the change in his eyes was instant.

He relaxed and nodded.

Celise turned back to Shade and kept watching the screen. No new surprises arose. The device went black after about a minute, and she pulled it away from his skin. "Done. You can dress now."

He untied the T-shirt from his head. "Any news?" He slid his arms into the sleeves, covering his impressive muscular frame.

"Only the same warning as usual. You and Phoebe can go on your holiday."

Shade put his hand on her arm. "Thanks, Celise. I really appreciate—"

A roar filled the room, and before she could react, Wind lunged at the other cyborg. He pushed him against the wall. Fury shone in his eyes, and they seemed to shine stronger than usual.

The sight sent a cold chill down her spine. She'd never seem Wind like this. The calmness he always radiated was gone without a trace. Rage and darkness lingered in his expression now.

He was ready to kill.

Shade's eyes widened but didn't fight back. He allowed Wind to slam him against the wall.

Phoebe gasped loudly and placed her hands against her mouth.

"Shit," Faye said and jumped back.

Celise stood frozen. Her heart pounded as she watched the two cyborgs, seconds away from ending up in a fight. Everything within her screamed to separate them, but if she tried, she'd end up with a broken bone or two. They both were a lot stronger than her.

"Don't touch her!" Wind roared. His voice was filled with threatening promises.

141

"Calm down," Shade said. "You're not a newborn cyborg. You *know* I'd never hurt Celise."

His rage seemed to intensify. His grip on Shade's T-shirt became white knuckled. "She's mine!"

Shade placed his hand on Wind's arm. "I know she's yours, and I promise, I won't touch her again. I forgot one touch would set you off." He frowned. "You're feeling primitive, aren't you?"

Wind only nodded with clenched jaws. His mouth was a hard line.

"We both know what that's like, how difficult it is to control, but I need you to take a deep breath. This is not you."

Wind didn't flinch, but hesitation lit up on his face.

Shade slowly grabbed his fist. "Let go, and allow me to move away from Celise. That's what you want, isn't it?"

Wind blinked. He didn't move for a while. Then he released his grip fast, as if he'd been burnt. The anger seemed to vanish with it. Guilt radiated from his gaze instead. "I'm sorry. I didn't mean too—"

Shade nodded. "I know. Is it like when you were newborn?"

Wind shook his head. "No, it's worse. The anger awakened when Phoebe called and it has just grown. The more I thought about Celise touching you, the more enraged I became." His gaze turned to her. "I think what

142

Jade warned us about is happening."

"What do you mean?" Celise asked.

"I'm bonding with you even if I'm still bound to Diane. I feel it happening."

She held her breath for two seconds, as hope awakened inside her. "Does that mean—?"

Wind smiled. "I'm starting to feel more than friendship. I think I just proved that."

His beautiful, shining eyes looked at her, and in them, she saw truth. He wasn't lying. Wind saw her in a new light. Slowly, he started to see her the way she'd always wanted — with love.

He approached her, and Celise rested her hand against his cheek, looking deep into his eyes. The love she had for him blossomed within her.

He pulled her closer, wrapping his arm around her.

Faye cleared her throat. "You have an audience, sweethearts, but don't worry. I don't mind watching."

Heat flushed Celise's face when she noticed everyone had their eyes on them.

"It looks like your bonding is going in the right direction," Phoebe said and smiled. "I'm happy for you."

"Thank you," Wind said. He seemed happy too, even if he'd been angry moments ago.

Shade moved to stand by Phoebe's side, and Celise couldn't have been more grateful. He and Wind had to avoid each other when she was around until the bond was set. Even if they were friends, Wind wouldn't be able to control himself.

"I think we should go," Celise said. She put the scanner inside her bag and threw the bag's strap over her shoulder. "I'd love to stay and chat, but—" She glanced at Wind.

Phoebe nodded. "I understand."

"Have a great holiday, you two," Celise said. "See you later, Faye."

Faye gave them a wicked grin and nodded.

It wasn't a shocker where her friend's mind was heading, but Celise wasn't going to give her the pleasure of hearing more about their bonding. Instead, she grabbed Wind's hand, and they headed for the front door.

A joy she'd never dared to feel before wrapped around her like a warm blanket.

He was becoming hers.

CHAPTER 17

Wild opened the door to his and Diane's house.

Celise followed him inside.

He held her hand in a firm grip, almost as if he didn't want to let her go. She loved it. His touch made her feel cozy inside. She couldn't help but smile as they walked up the stairs to the second floor.

Something amazing was happening.

Wind had never looked at her the way he was now. He'd been driving and gazing at her from time to time with a mysterious smile, studying her, evaluating the situation.

Wind led her toward Diane's room. He didn't knock before opening the door.

Diane was still sitting on the balcony, reading a book. She lowered it when they joined her. "How did it go?"

Wind let go of Celise's hand and approached Diane. "It

went great."

"Well, that depends on how you look at it. At least Wind and Shade are in one piece," Celise said.

Diane frowned. She looked worried for a moment, but then her eyes sparkled with excitement. "The bond was triggered. Shade touched you, and Wind didn't like it." It was a statement, not a question.

Wind fell on his knees in front of Diane and placed his hands on her legs. "It's happening, my love. I can feel it awakening. I'm falling in love with Celise." There was so much pride in his voice.

Celise was unable to speak. Her heart skipped as his words sank in. Hearing him say it was like a dream coming true. The warm feeling in her limbs increased, and her love for him exploded in her chest. A tear of joy ran down her cheek.

Wind pinned her with a gaze, and she saw it.

The love he spoke of.

It really was there, sparkling in his mesmerizing eyes, and all she wanted was to hug him and say thank you, but she didn't move, because that would've been childish. Instead, she hugged herself.

A feeling of peace filled her.

For the first time ever, Celise wasn't afraid to love him. Before she had always pushed her feelings aside, because they could never be, but now, she could finally let everything out.

Diane smiled. "I'm happy to hear that. Are you all right with it?"

Wind nodded. "My feelings for Celise are growing fast. They've increased remarkably, even during the short ride back here. I think it'll continue at this pace until I'm completely bound to her."

"And what about your bond to me?"

"It's still there, as strong as always."

Diane's smile faded. "Oh. That means—"

"That I'll be bound to the both of you for some time."

Celise didn't miss Diane's unspoken question when she made eye contact with her. She worried what would happen if Wind remained bound to both of them. Was it even possible for a cyborg to remain bound to two women? And what would happen if Diane suddenly died?

She hoped with all her heart her friend's passing was in the far future, but judging by her weak appearance, pale skin, and tired eyes, it was only a matter of time.

At worst, Diane had weeks remaining.

"I know Jade forbid it, but I want to spend one day with the both of you." Wind's gaze lingered between them with a glimpse of hope. "Just one day. That's all I'm asking. One day without restrictions of what is right or wrong for me to do. I want to be able to touch you both whenever I want, and how much I want."

Silence filled the balcony.

Celise and Diane exchanged gazes again.

What her friend wanted didn't escape her notice. There was so much hope in her tired eyes, it almost broke Celise's heart.

Diane wanted badly to spend one last day with Wind. Once the bond was transferred, she'd never be able to touch him intimately again.

He would always have feelings for Diane, but his need for her would be gone. Diane would have to spend her final days alone, with no one to hold her or love her ... didn't matter how long she had left.

Celise took a deep breath. "Let's do it."

Hesitation lingered in Diane's eyes. "What if what we have accomplished so far disappears if Wind and I touch?

"I don't think it will," Wind said.

"How can you be sure?"

He gave her a comforting smile. "Because I feel it."

Diane placed her hand on his cheek as happiness filled her gaze. "I'd love nothing more but spend one last day with you." She leaned in and kissed him.

Wind wrapped his arms around Diane and deepened the kiss. His tongue mingled with hers, and he groaned as he closed his eyes. Happiness radiated from him, too.

Celise didn't move as she watched them kiss. To her surprise, it didn't cause an emotional havoc within her seeing them like this. Instead, she was glad for their sake.

They needed this.

One last time ...

CHAPTER 18

Celise stared at the white canvas in front of her. She held a brush, dipped in blue paint, ready to start, but hesitation lingered in her whole body. She was so out of her league. She'd never been interested in painting. She could barely draw a stick figure with straight lines, for heaven's sake.

Wind's arms wrapped around her waist, making her jump and lose her concentration. "Don't look so terrified. It's just a canvas. It's not going to eat you."

"I'm not so sure about that."

He chuckled near her ear, making her shiver with anticipation when his warm breath grazed her skin. "Remember what I said; light and gentle strokes with a steady hand, from one side to the other. It doesn't matter if you ruin the canvas. I have plenty more, so experiment as much as you want."

"I can't believe you're letting me do this."

"Why? I love having you here."

Heat rushed to her face. "You do?"

He rested his cheek against hers. "A fire is burning within me, and it's burning for you. It surprises me how strong it is considering that just two days ago, I couldn't even imagine this. You were my friend and nothing more, but now, ever since we came back from Shade and Phoebe's, my body is responding. Do you feel it?" He pulled her hips back against him.

Celise tensed when a hard bulge pressed against her bottom. She stood frozen, staring at the canvas as surprise sang inside her.

"That's all because of you." Wind's voice was barely a whisper.

"But yesterday, you couldn't—" Her lower lip trembled.

"That was yesterday."

Diane, working on her own painting next to them, chuckled as her brush swept on the canvas with grace. "Are you starting to understand what you're getting, Celise? If you think this is how far he can go, you're up for a surprise. Remember, Wind has a high sex-drive. You'll have to learn how to enjoy it because right now you remind me of a stiff teenage girl who wants so much, but is too afraid to take the next step." She set her brush down. "He's yours, Celise. Don't be afraid of his touch."

"I'm ... I'm not used to this." She could barely control

her voice.

"Don't worry. I'll make you relax." Wind's hands slid up and down her arms.

Celise gulped. She'd been with him last night, but it still was like he was touching her for the first time. Right now, it seemed like *he'd* get used to her faster than she'd get used to him. "Shouldn't we be painting?"

"We can take a break." Wind reached for the palette in her hand.

"But ... you wanted to spend time with Diane. Shouldn't you do that?"

"I *am* spending time with her, and you. We've already been having fun for several hours."

That was true. They'd talked, even danced, and eaten delicious food that they'd prepared together, and during that time, Wind had touched Diane a great deal.

He'd caressed her, and even pressed her against the wall while smothering her with kisses.

Diane had enjoyed it without a doubt, but she hadn't been able to hide her fatigue. She'd often needed to take a break.

Celise had watched them with warmth in her heart. The jealousy she usually felt wasn't there anymore. Instead, she was relieved that they got one last chance to be together.

Wind hadn't left her feeling abandoned. He'd made sure to be near her too, but he hadn't tried to kiss her, and she didn't blame him. Instead, he'd wrapped his arms around her every other minute, caressed her, or given her a smile.

Celise allowed him to take the palette away. She turned to face him as he placed it on the table.

He returned to her with a grin, wrapping his arms around her again. "We haven't tried kissing since this morning. Do you want to try now?"

Celise swallowed. "I don't want to hurt you."

"I'll pull away if I feel the slightest resistance from my bond."

She could only nod. Her hands trembled as she hoped for the best.

Wind went slowly this time, really slowly. He pressed his lips to hers, then pulled back. He did so three times before he met her gaze. His aluminum-shining eyes studied her with a hint of insecurity.

Maybe he was afraid of the pain. It wouldn't surprise her. She'd seen how much discomfort it'd caused him. He'd become more and more cautious.

Nothing seemed to be happening, so when he pressed his lips against hers a fourth time, he prolonged the kiss.

Celise wasn't able to hold back a moan when his tongue carefully touched her bottom lip. She closed her eyes, battling with herself, trying to hold back, but everything inside her screamed not to deny what her body yearned for.

She raised her arms to wrap them around him but lowered them again when she realized what she was doing. She couldn't be the one to lead. She had to allow Wind to take things in his pace, but his touch set her on fire. She couldn't escape it. She'd never been as aroused as she'd been these last few days.

Wind chuckled against her mouth. Of course, he noticed.

"It's not funny," she growled.

"No, but it's cute." He grabbed her behind with a firm grip, pushing her against his bulge.

Celise squeaked, staring at him with surprise.

His eyes glowed stronger than usual, and it was impossible to miss his arousal. It was so different from yesterday. He seemed eager to touch her. The way his hands traveled all over her, almost devouring her gave him away. It was as if he couldn't get enough.

"Let's try to kiss for real," he said.

Celise opened her mouth to ask if that was such a good idea, but Wind didn't give her a chance. Instead, he claimed her mouth with his as if he owned it. He grabbed her neck with his strong hand to keep her from escaping.

She'd never expected him to do that. And she'd never expected him to be so ... hungry, so willing. He was actually kissing her, and his bond wasn't objecting. When he brushed his tongue against hers, Celise wasn't able to hold back anymore.

She allowed her body to take over. The surroundings disappeared as she wrapped her arms around him, showing Wind how much she needed him. A slight fear of him pulling away lingered in her mind, but she calmed with each passing second when it didn't happen.

His bond had finally accepted them kissing.

He pulled away with a grin on his lips and met her gaze.

Celise gasped. "Wind, your eyes ..."

Diane approached. She seemed unaffected by what'd taken place in front of her. Instead, she grinned as she looked at him.

He frowned at them both. "What do you see?"

"Your eyes are glowing more than usual," Celise said. "The glow is strong, almost blinding. I've never seen anything like it, but it's beautiful." Her words came out as whispers. She stared, mesmerized by the sight.

"How are you feeling?" Diane asked him.

"I feel fine, but I'm aroused." Wind suddenly gasped and grabbed their hands. He opened his mouth, but nothing came out.

Worry filled Celise. "Is everything all right?"

He shook his head as if to shake something off of him. "My bond ... it's ..."

A fire she hadn't seen before shone in his eyes. It seemed to overwhelm him, making him look drunk. Drunk on passion and desire.

He moaned and rubbed his cheek against hers. "I need you." He glanced at Diane. "I need you, too."

Diane and Celise exchanged gazes.

CHAPTER 19

Wind closed the door as they tumbled into the bedroom. He dimmed the light, making the room cozy before going to the player on the wall. He waved his hand in front of it, and slow romantic music started to play from the speakers.

He assessed Diane and Celise.

They both watched him with obviously mixed emotions.

Diane, even if she looked tired, seemed enthralled. She didn't seem to mind this at all. If it helped him to bind with Celise, she'd gladly do it. That meant a lot to him.

He rested his gaze on the shy doctor by Diane's side.

They were like night and day. Diane stood determined, while Celise barely dared to look him in the eyes. Her cheeks were flushed, and she rang her hands as if she didn't know what to do with them.

The bond screamed inside him, but in a good way. He'd been aroused for a while now. He hadn't been able to shake it off, and he didn't want to, either. Instead, Wind wanted to explore everything Celise was willing to give and see where it'd take them. But he needed Diane by his side, too. Even if the bond was all right with Celise now, it still wanted Diane.

He approached them. "Are you both sure you want to do this?"

Diane nodded, but Celise hesitated.

He grabbed her hand. "My bond's ready for you, but I need Diane here. It won't work without her."

She swallowed, appearing to study him for a few seconds before she nodded as well. "I'm good. I can do this." She licked her lips. "I'm just nervous."

Wind relaxed and tried to smile. "So am I." He placed her hand against his chest. "Do you feel that? My heart is pounding like crazy."

She gave a nervous giggle. "Mine too."

His smile widened. "That means we're on the same page."

Diane placed her hands on each of their shoulders. "Let everything come naturally."

Celise blushed deeper, lowering her gaze.

Wind found her shyness cute, but he saw strength, too.

Taking care of many cyborgs as one of MedAct's doctors had to be challenging, considering that they probably weren't always that cooperative.

Besides ... she was still here ...

He admired her for that.

Wind pulled them closer, closing his eyes as they put their foreheads against each others. He allowed the calm atmosphere in the room fill him, hoping they felt it as well.

He wanted this. He *really* wanted this.

He'd barely dared to imagine this day. When he'd tried to imagine Celise naked in his arms a few days ago, his bond had protested and caused him pain. But now, everything was different. Now, Wind wanted nothing more but to see Celise naked underneath him.

Something pulled him toward her. He couldn't get away from the thought that it was love. He knew love, and what he felt for her reminded of it. It'd been there ever since Phoebe had called, and it grew stronger with each passing minute.

The door to make her his bound one had finally been opened.

His desire for Diane scorched inside him as well. He wanted her touch to make him burn. She always managed to drive him wild with her kisses and caresses.

Wind suspected how this was going to end. Once the first flash happened, he'd be bound to both of them.

He didn't mind.

He raised his hands, slowly gliding them up the women's backs, heading for their necks. He caressed them, messaging with slow but steady pressure.

Diane moaned, and he didn't miss the pleased smile on her lips.

Celise's eyes were closed. She seemed tense, but he'd make her relax. He'd make sure she'd melt in his arms, and before the night was over, her shyness would be nothing but a memory.

"There's only us here," Wind whispered in her ear.

She gazed up at him. Her nervousness shone strongly in her eyes, but she didn't back away. She was ready to face this.

Wind pressed his lips to hers without letting go of Diane. He kept caressing her as he kissed Celise.

It was a new, but exciting experience. He wanted to go the whole way, but would he be able to? He couldn't wait to find out. It awakened his curiosity and eagerness.

Diane's presence pulled at him. He went for her lips but didn't let Celise feel abandoned. He caressed her back, showing her he was there with her.

His original bound one's kiss was filled with passion and desire. She claimed his lips with a wild need he hadn't seen in her for several months.

His heart clenched. He understood what it meant.

This was their last time together.

With that realization singing in his whole being, he wrapped his arms around Diane, pulling her hard against his chest. Her lips tasted sweet and warm. They were just as soft and amazing as they'd always been. He loved kissing her, and he'd miss it.

Two hands landed on his butt. Wind peeked behind him and saw Celise.

Her hands glided toward his hips, slowly exploring him. She rested her cheek against his back and took a deep but shaky breath.

Her embrace told him everything.

It whispered of the love she had for him as her fingers moved around. He couldn't wait to find out what else she'd do. The combination of her touch and Diane's kisses was intoxicating. They were all over him, and he loved every second of it. His bond couldn't agree more.

It wanted more.

A lot more ... and so did he.

Diane didn't shy away with her desire.

At this moment, Wind was grateful he wore sweatpants because he'd never been this hard before. It was almost painful. Even his balls ached. His whole body longed for a release, and his ladies didn't seem to mind giving him one.

He grabbed Diane's shirt to take it off her, but she stopped him. Surprise hit him, and he raised an eyebrow as he glanced at her.

"Tonight is all about you, my love. You can take care of us later, when your eyes have flashed."

Wind opened his mouth to object. That didn't sound fair. He wanted to make it good for them, too.

Celise interrupted him before he even got a chance to say a single word.

"I agree," she said against his back. "We need that flash, and it'll be more difficult if you have to focus on us as well."

"But—"

Diane placed a finger against his lips. "Shh, close your eyes and relax, my love. Just feel, and allow us to make you feel good."

To silence his protest wasn't easy, but he understood. He closed his eyes and allowed them to take over.

Diane helped him out of his shirt. Goosebumps awakened on his skin, but he wasn't freezing. It was excitement.

He'd never given in this completely before. Every time he and Diane had been together, they'd always made sure they were both truly satisfied at the end, but this time, he wasn't allowed to touch.

Wind actually looked forward to *them* being in charge.

He promised himself he'd make it up to the both of them later.

Diane's hands caressed his naked skin. They were a little cold, but it didn't take long for her to warm up on his feverish body. She helped herself, touching him all over without holding back.

It made him groan, awakening a desire to touch her, but if he tried, she'd stop him. He didn't doubt that. Once Diane had made up her mind, it was set.

This was all about him.

His focus turned to Celise as her hands started exploring new areas of him. Her shaky but determined fingers traveled to his front, slowly slipping inside his pants.

Wind gasped from the unexpected move. He'd hoped she'd be braver, but he hadn't expected *this*. His bond cheered when she wrapped her small fingers around his cock, making him tremble all over. "Celise," he groaned.

Her hand stilled and tensed.

"No, don't stop," he said. "I'm fine. The bond isn't hurting me."

She inhaled a breath, and her grip tightened, making him shiver. His knees weakened. He'd never imagined it would feel this good as she worked him with slow but steady moves. He thrust his hips to the pace of her hand.

A thin coat of sweat broke out on his skin as he leaned against Diane to remain standing. He was able to look her in the eyes and was brought back from his haze of lust when he expected to see disapproval on her face, but there were no such emotion.

Instead, she was smiling. Her eyes were filled with hope, but the small pinch of sadness didn't pass him by.

Celise's amazing hand and gentle fingers made him lose his grip on reality again, sliding him back into the haze of lust. He'd never believed she had it in her, but maybe there was another side to his doctor he wasn't familiar with.

"That feels so good," he groaned.

Diane's hands caressed his chest. Her tongue grazed his nipple, and her hand played with the other, spiking his arousal.

He couldn't take it anymore.

Wind shoved down his pants and stepped out of them. He grabbed Celise and kissed her as madness and desire slowly took over.

Something new was happening to him, but he couldn't figure out on what. His bond screamed at him to take them both, and his eyes started to feel warm. It was a strange sensation.

"Lay down," Diane said to him as she pulled the comforter away from the bed.

He did as she asked, but he didn't let go of Celise. He couldn't. He *had* to be close to her. He'd scream if she moved away.

"I'll go first, just in case," Diane said and stripped out of her pants and underwear.

Celise gave a sharp nod as she sat down by his side, looking into his eyes with longing and desire. Her chest rose and sank fast, and her cheeks were flushed.

She didn't tremble anymore, and her nerves seemed gone, but he didn't miss the underlying apprehension. He didn't blame her. Who knew what would happen once he got inside her. Maybe his bond would flip and go completely crazy on him.

That meant he risked hurting her.

His attention shot back to Diane when she straddled him. Anticipation awakened. He was ready to burst. He watched her as she placed herself above his cock. She grabbed it and slowly guided him right.

Wind groaned and buckled his back as she sank down on him, taking him in inch by inch. She was wet and ready for him. The warmth from her welcoming core made his head spin. He so loved this.

He squeezed Celise's hand, barely noticing that his grip tightened as Diane adapted to his size.

Wind pulled Celise over him; he needed to kiss her. He found her lips and his hand search for her breast, not caring anymore if this was all about him. He *had* to touch her, and Celise didn't stop him. Instead, she made it easier for him by taking off her shirt.

With one smooth move, he pulled out her breast from

the bra and squeezed it in his big hand, rubbing her nipple between his fingers.

She shivered, and a moan left her lips.

It pleased him.

His bond hummed with satisfaction. He was doing the right thing. He could continue. His bond wouldn't interfere. There was no doubt about that now.

Celise's kiss and Diane slowly riding him was pure bliss, sending him into oblivion.

Wind closed his eyes.

The grasp of reality slowly slipped away as passion took over.

CHAPTER 20

Wind seemed lost in his own pleasure. His eyes were closed, and his mouth slightly open. His body quivered from time to time, and he clenched his knuckles as his breathing became deeper.

Celise smiled to herself as she watched him lying on the bed taking everything she and Diane gave him. They were all over him. Kissing, licking, touching as Diane slowly fucked him.

She didn't mind any of it.

Not anymore.

Somewhere along the way, her nerves and shyness had abandoned her. Desire and longing had taken over.

She'd never been able to touch him the way she touched him now. She filled her starved yearning with pleasurable kisses and seductive caresses, and Wind enjoyed everything. His bond seemed to behave as well.

"I think he's ready for you now," Diane said. Her eyes were glassy, and her cheeks were flushed.

Celise tensed. "Are you sure?"

Diane smiled. "I'm sure, and if anything happens, I'm right here."

She tensed her jaw. "You know you can't stop him, or save me if something goes wrong, right?"

Diane's smile faded. She remained silent before she turned to Wind, who still was lost in his own little world. "Look at him. Look at his eyes. They're closed, and yet, you can see the glow coming from underneath the eyelids." Her smile returned. "His bond is waiting for you. Waiting for that first flash."

Celise did as Diane said, and indeed, there was a glow behind his eyelids.

Her friend climbed off Wind, and put on her panties and pants. Her fatigue shone right through. It almost seemed like a miracle that she'd been able to do this.

"Are you all right?" Celise asked.

"Don't worry about me." She nodded toward the cyborg. "Take care of him." She sat down on a chair next to the bed.

Celise swallowed, and her gaze traveled to Wind's jutting cock; proud and ready.

Waiting for *her*.

The sight of him made her vaginal walls clench from

168

need. She was finally going to experience what she'd dreamt of for so long.

She swallowed and stood, taking off her pants and underwear before slipping over his legs. Her heart galloped as she grabbed him, feeling the thick and warm organ pulse in her hand.

Wind groaned and threw his head back. His eyes were still closed. His fingers grabbed the linens and held on tight. The glow behind his eyelids intensified.

She was more than ready for him. After watching him with Diane, and kissing, touching him, her body demanded him. She wanted him badly, and all she could do was pray this worked.

Celise took a deep breath and exhaled.

This was it.

She hovered above him, lingering for a second before lowering her upper body and slowly allowing him to penetrate her.

A wave of pleasure hit her when he stretched her inch by inch. He was hard as stone but warm and smooth. She felt him pulse inside her, making her moan again. The amazing feeling made her forget Diane was watching.

Celise tossed her chin up as he filled her completely. It was a shock to her system to finally have him like is. It made her tremble as the pleasure became almost overwhelming. Her love for him only intensified it. She forgot the possible dangers as she raised her body and sank down on him again, slowly building a rhythm.

Wind's breathing increased. He writhed underneath her, unable to lie still. He jerked and let out a cry, as if in pain.

Celise froze in place, staring at him.

Was something wrong?

His hands grabbed her hips, and his eyes flew open. He gnashed his teeth. Anger radiated from him, a determination and hunger so strong it made her gasp.

Diane stood. "Wind?"

Wind sat up so fast both Celise and Diane winced with a load gasp. He wrapped his arms around Celise, and with one swift move, flipped them around.

She squeaked when she landed on her back on the bed. The intense light in his eyes made her gape at him. He didn't give her time to ask what was happening. Instead, he parted her legs and plunged inside.

His starved thrust made Celise lose her breath for a second. His strength dawned on her. Wind's sanity seemed to be slipping, and there was nothing she could do but hold on.

He thrust inside her over and over again, and each time, harder and faster. The whole bed shook, the headboard banged against the wall. His grunts of passion and frustration echoed in her head as his pelvis slammed against hers.

"Shit!" Diane rushed to the bed. "I've never seen him like this. Celise, are you all right?"

"I'm ... fine." She could barely speak. Her voice shook, ecstasy building. It was impossible to stop it. Pleasure approached with each determined thrust.

Celise wrapped her arms around him and bit his shoulder as her orgasm finally clutched her. Her body shook underneath him, and she was unable to hold back her shout.

Wind didn't stop. He continued his relentless treatment of her oversensitive body, wrapping his arms around her possessively.

There was no way for her to get away. Nothing would make him stop, but she didn't mind. This was the most amazing thing she'd ever experienced, feeling him losing control completely.

He raised his upper-body and threw back his head. He roared; his body jerked from his release, filling her with his warm seed.

An intense and blinding light flashed from Wind's eyes.

Sweaty and warm, he collapsed on Celise. He remained still. Their heavy breathing filled the room.

"Oh, my God!" Diane laughed. "Did you see that? His eyes flashed."

Celise stared at the ceiling. She was exhausted, hot,

but had never felt better. She could barely believe what'd just happened. She wanted to laugh, but lay still instead, enjoying the moment. She almost wanted to purr when his organ throbbed inside her.

She'd seen his eyes flash too, and that had been the best part.

The bond had been initiated.

The worst was behind them. Jade had said getting the second and third flash would be easier once the first one had happened.

She grabbed Wind's arms. "Wind, you have to move. It's getting difficult to breathe."

He didn't react.

Diane's smile faded. "Wind?"

Nothing.

"Help me roll him over," Celise said. Worry awakened within her.

Diane grabbed his arm and shoulder, and pulled.

Celise pushed at his chest. "Damn, he's heavy." A last wave of pleasure went through her when he slipped out of her.

They managed to get him on his back and stared at his face.

"What the hell?" Diane frowned.

Wind seemed far away, his eyes stared at the ceiling with an empty gaze.

"Is this supposed to be happening?" Diane asked.

"I have no idea, but probably. Let's wait and see."

Diane looked her over. "How are you feeling?"

"He didn't hurt me, but I didn't expect him to be that wild."

Diane grinned. "He usually isn't, at least not like *that*, but I can promise you, he'll take you on plenty more wild rides."

Heat traveled to her cheeks. "I hope so." Her smile faded. "Are *you* ... all right?"

"Just tired. Before, I could go on for hours. Now, a few minutes wear me out." She huffed. "I guess that's just the way it is."

Celise cleared her throat. "I meant ... seeing me and Wind ..."

Diane grabbed her arm. "Deep down, I feel sadness. It's unavoidable, but don't worry. I'm fine. I really am. He's safe now, and that's what's important."

Celise took a deep breath and nodded.

Wind blinked and groaned.

Their attention immediately turned to him.

He slowly sat up, looking at them with confusion written all over his face. "My eyes flashed. I'm bound to both of you now, but I never expected it to feel like this." He placed his hand on his chest.

Diane moved closer. "Tell us."

He hesitated. "It's a mess, honestly. My bond is confused but thrilled at the same time. I feel drawn to the both of you." Wind's eyes went suddenly wide as he winced and gasped. Then, he reached for them, resting a palm on Diane's cheek, and the other on Celise's. He chuckled and glanced at Celise as realization seemed to hit him. "I love you." His gaze turned to his first bound one. "I love you both."

Celise exchanged a look with Diane, and they both smiled.

"And we love you," Diane said.

Celise nodded and dried away a tear of joy. She'd never believed she'd hear him say those three words to her. It was almost as if a miracle had just happened, and she couldn't get enough of the happiness that filled every part of her body.

Wind wrapped his arms around them, gently kissing each mouth. "Then how about me taking care of *you* now?" He gave them a wicked grin.

CHAPTER 21

Diane opened the door to the bedroom as quietly as possible so she wouldn't wake Wind and Celise. She gave them one last look and smiled. Her cyborg was spooning Celise, and they both looked happy in their sleep.

She was happy for them, too. His eyes had finally flashed. He loved Celise now. Just two more flashes and his bond would fully belong to her, and where things went from there was up to them.

Emptiness washed over her, filling her and shoving the contentment away.

She wouldn't be a part of their lives then.

She'd be alone.

Diane took a deep breath and tried not to think about it. All was for the best.

It'd been an amazing night. She'd been in Wind's arms many times, and so had Celise. He'd taken care of them both, just like he'd promised.

He'd loved them in many different ways, and they'd loved him back. She'd forgotten how many times she'd come, or how many times Celise had.

They'd given him pleasure as well ... and she'd never forget the sight of him when he was lost in passion. He'd been so beautiful in his own desire.

Eventually, they'd all fallen asleep. It actually amazed her that she'd been able to go on for so long, considering how exhausted she'd been after just a few minutes in the beginning, but she'd taken a break whenever she'd needed, and that had done the trick. Besides, she'd wanted to be with him badly. Her determination had helped her through the night, her last night with Wind.

Their time together seemed to have changed Celise as well. She'd been tense and shy in the beginning, but the further things had gone, the more she'd relaxed. Diane hoped it'd remain like that. It suited her better.

Diane closed the bedroom door and headed for the guest room where she'd slept the night before. She sat down on her favorite armchair on the balcony and covered her legs with the blanket she'd left there.

It was still early morning, but the mild summer breeze was pleasurable against her feverish skin.

She didn't feel well. The amazing night had taken its toll, but it'd been worth it. Her pulse was up, and that worried her. The headache and the dizziness were constant reminders; she was only getting worse. The fever burned brightly since she'd woken, and showed no signs of going away, but it wasn't because of the heat of passion as the night before, it was pain.

A tear ran down her cheek, and fear grabbed her.

She wanted to live. There were still so many things she wanted to do, but judging by her condition, she didn't have the time. Diane could only *hope.*

The image of Wind's handsome face and kind eyes flashed by in her mind. How she loved that man. To her, he was so much more than a cyborg.

He was her *everything.*

She'd never loved anyone as she loved him; that was why she was doing this, making sure he'd survive her death.

It filled her with joy *and* sadness watching him with Celise. One side of her wanted to chase her friend away, to order her to stop touching Wind, while the other wanted her to stay.

Diane had to put her own feelings aside, but it was difficult. It had been the greatest challenge of her life, but somehow she'd been able to go through all this.

Just two more flashes and Wind's bond would be Celise's.

He'd finally be safe.

Agony in her chest intensified. She should go to the kitchen and grab her pills, but she was so tired. So incredibly tired.

Diane frowned. She'd never been this tired before.

Wind's beautiful and understanding eyes filled her mind once again, and she smiled.

It was strange, but she wasn't afraid anymore.

So tired ...

CHAPTER 22

Gentle kisses and caresses awakened Celise from slumber. She smiled when Wind nipped the shell of her ear. The heat from his body and the warm covers made her feel cozy and safe.

"Good morning, my dear," Wind said. "Did you sleep well?"

"Mmm," she murmured. "How about you?" She rolled over to face him.

His aluminum-looking eyes shone the way they always did, but now, they also sparkled with happiness. "I slept like a baby."

She chuckled. "That's good." Celise moved a little bit. "My muscles ache."

He grinned. "It's from all the action last night."

Heat traveled to her face. "It was amazing."

Wind cupped her cheek and looked her deep into the eyes. "I can't believe we've come this far. The bond has initiated, and I feel love for you now. My instincts to protect you are through the roof."

Her heart started to beat faster as she swallowed. "And Diane?"

"My feelings for her haven't changed. I don't think they will. Does that bother you?"

Celise winced, couldn't help it. "No, of course not. She'll always be a part of you."

He placed himself on top of her, stroking her face. "Have you thought about what we should do once I'm completely bound to you?"

"What do you mean?" His touch awakened goosebumps on her skin.

"Like where we shall live?" Wind kissed her cheek.

She closed her eyes, enjoying the sensation. "Um ... I honestly haven't thought about it."

He frowned, seemed surprised. "Really?"

"I guess I've been too focused on making the transfer, but now when you ask, I have an idea."

Her cyborg leaned down and kissed her throat. "Tell me."

"Let's stay here."

Wind stilled before he met her gaze. "Here?"

"Yes. Diane will be alone. I don't want that. She's my

friend, and I think it will mean a lot to her to still have you around during her final time in life. Besides ... this is your home."

Disbelief colored his eyes. "You'd give up your home to live here with me?"

Celise swallowed. "You don't want that? My house is nothing special. This house is a masterpiece. Wherever I look, I see traces of you both. You've both put your touch and time into everything here. This house breathes you and Diane."

His eyes watered as a wide smile spread on his lips. "You'd really do that for me?"

"Of course. I love you."

He leaned down, kissing her gently. "I love you, too." He parted her legs, and without much effort, found her entrance.

She closed her eyes again and moaned when he pushed inside. It was pure bliss, and each thrust was like a sensual stroke at her core.

He wrapped her in his arms, loved her slowly, building up her desire. His silent groans tickled her ear, blinding her with pleasure.

Despite their wild night, it didn't take much for her to climax. She doubted it ever would with him. When her inner muscles tightened around him, Wind increased his speed. His breathing deepened, and seconds later, his groans mixed with her cry. His warm release filled her, and she loved it.

He remained still afterward, catching his breath.

Celise gasped. "We never used protection."

Wind raised his head. "Don't worry. If you get pregnant, I'll love the child just as much as I love you and Diane."

Relief filled her. "You and Diane never wanted children?"

"Diane said she considered herself too old for children when she created me, but she never put into my programming that I wouldn't want any."

She smiled. Having a child with him was a dream she'd never dared to imagine, but now when that future was possible, she allowed hope to fill her.

He rolled over to his side. "I'll go and clean up, and then I'll check up on Diane. She must've gone back to her room while we were sleeping." Wind gave her one last kiss before he left the bed, walking naked toward the bathroom door.

Celise grinned as she watched him go. A firm behind and smooth skin greeted her sight, making her lick her lips. She'd never grow tired of looking at his amazing body. It made her happy to know he wasn't ashamed of showing himself to her.

It only took him a few minutes to get ready, and once he left the bedroom, Celise got up and washed as fast as she could. She wanted to spend every possible moment with Wind *and* Diane.

She was just about to join them when someone knocked on the front door.

Wind and Diane didn't seem to have heard it, so she approached the door, and opened it. Celise raised an eyebrow when Faye smiled at her. "Faye? What're you doing here?"

She shrugged and entered the house. "I was bored. Phoebe and Shade have gone on their holiday, and I figured you guys could spend a few hours with me."

"You know we're in the middle of transferring Wind's bond to me, right?"

"Of course, and I doubt a few hours with me will disrupt your scheme."

Celise sighed. Faye was right. There was no reason for her to leave. It was just that she wanted to spend some time with Wind and Diane, just the three of them, now that the first flash had occurred.

"How are things going, by the way?" Faye asked.

"Fine." She closed the front door. "The first flash has happened. So the worst should be behind us."

A wide smile spread on Faye's face, slowly turning into a wicked grin. "So how was it? The sex? It must've been one kind of ride."

Heat traveled to Celise's face, but she couldn't help her

smile. "I don't think I have to spell it for you, do I?"

"That amazing, huh?" She chuckled.

Celise nodded. It sure had been amazing. The best day of her life. All her restrictions had gone through the door. She'd finally been allowed to love Wind the way she'd always wanted to.

Next time she'd wrap her arms around him, he wouldn't feel pain, and wouldn't turn away. Instead, he'd pull her to him, kiss her, and make her happy.

A loud thump came from the second floor, as if something had landed hard on the floor.

Celise and Faye tensed, looking at each other.

"What was that?" Faye asked.

"I don't know."

A roar of terror and agony filled the air.

A cold chill hit her chest. "Wind." Without a second thought, she ran up the stairs.

Faye followed her.

A million thoughts traveled through Celise's mind. Had furniture fallen over Wind? Had he broken something? Or had he just hit his foot against something? No, she doubted that. The thump hadn't been loud, but his scream had filled her with fear.

What if ...?

Celise yanked the door open. The scene that greeted her tore her heart out.

It was worse than she'd dared to imagine.

Wind sat on the floor with Diane in his arms. The armchair had been knocked over. Diane wasn't moving. Her eyes were closed, her skin pale as snow.

He looked up when they ran into the room. His eyes were filled with tears, and gut-wrenching pain was written all over his face. His chin trembled. "She's dead."

"Oh my God," Faye gasped.

Celise crouched down next to Wind and Diane. She checked for her friend's pulse, but there was none.

She really was gone.

The beautiful morning had turned into a surreal nightmare. Sorrow surged through her. She was unable to stop her tears.

Wind held her gaze. "Celise ... help me." His voice was barely a whisper, and his body started to tremble even more.

She froze. The light in his shining eyes was fading. "What?"

"The bond ... I'm dying ..."

"But ... your eyes flashed."

"Not ... enough ..." He fell to his side, his body going slack as he closed his eyes and exhaled. Then, he suddenly started to shake so violently Celise feared he'd bite his tongue off.

"Shit," Faye gasped with wide eyes.

It didn't take long before sweat broke out on his skin. His face and throat turned red as he struggled with clenched fists.

Terror grabbed Celise as she stared at the man she loved, but she couldn't allow it to set. "Get my bag. It's in the bedroom."

Faye took off in an instance, and Celise grabbed Diane's cold body, moving her away from Wind. There was nothing she could do for her, but she could try to save Wind.

She wasn't going to lose him.

She was a doctor. She was the only one who *could* save him.

Celise scooted closer on her knees but knew it wasn't wise to touch him. He could hurt her with his inhuman strength in this condition, but it didn't seem like the shaking would stop anytime soon.

There was only one thing she could try until Faye returned.

With one swift move, she grabbed Wind by the neck and pressed one finger against his spine and another one just behind his right ear. Her pinky reached for that sensitive spot she was looking for, and when she found it, she pressed it.

He instantly stilled with closed eyes.

Faye stormed into the room and handed her the bag.

"What did you do?"

Celise searched through the bag as fast as she could. "Cyborgs have a unique nerve in their necks. If you know how to activate it, you can make them lose consciousness for a short while."

Her friend blinked. "I didn't know that. Why do they have it?"

"They're stronger, faster, and more intelligent than humans, so MedAct gave them a weak point." She pulled out the device she was looking for. She threw the bag away, pulled Wind's shirt up, and pressed it against his chest. Her heart was pounding as she scanned him. Her hands shook, and tears pushed from behind her eyes, but she kept them away. It was difficult to keep her emotions at bay, but she had to.

For Wind.

If she allowed panic and chaos rule her, he would die.

Celise couldn't stop her chin from trembling when she saw the result from the scan. "His bond to Diane is going amok." The words came out shaky. "That first flash with me is the only thing keeping him alive, but if his eyes don't flash two more times, he'll die anyway within a few hours."

"Then do something!"

She met Faye's desperate gaze, hopelessness filling her. "I can't force it, but I'll do everything I can. Somehow, I'll make his eyes flash again." She reached for Wind's face.

Without warning, he woke with a scream.

Faye jerked beside her.

The panic that radiated from him was impossible to miss. He scanned frantically around him before he flew to his feet, breathing heavily, and swaying as if he was drunk. He squeezed his eyes hard, trying to focus, but seemed unable to.

Celise climbed to her feet and grabbed his face. Seeing him in this state broke her heart. "Wind. I'm here. Look at me. Please, look at me ..."

He tried, but seconds later, his eyes glazed over. He pushed away and let out another agony filled scream. He wrapped his arms around his head, pulled his hair, and scratched his face as he curled up.

The sound devastated her from the inside out. It tore her apart, and she could barely imagine the pain he had to be in. She wasn't going to be able to save him.

Wind darted for the balcony.

Celise gasped. "Wind, no!"

But he didn't listen; he jumped.

Tears ran down her face as she and Faye ran up to the balcony. "Wind!" She looked down, feared she'd see him lying on the ground with broken limbs, but he was already on his feet, seemingly unhurt.

He darted off.

"Wind!"

CHAPTER 23

Pain burned inside Wind's chest. It tormented him to the deepest part of his soul. It filled him with a fear he'd never felt before.

He was dying.

His death had just been prolonged, thanks to his weak bond to Celise. It would keep him alive for just a little bit longer, but there was no way for him to escape death.

He ran as fast as he could. It wasn't important *where,* as the panic ate at him. It was a desperate attempt to get away from the agony and the shock that devastated his system.

The image of Diane sitting dead on the armchair had been burnt into his mind. An image he'd never be able to get away from.

The moment he'd seen her body, everything had changed.

Wind had been happy just minutes before, after the

most amazing night of his life, but when his bond had realized what'd happened, all hell had broken loose inside him.

His bound one was dead, and he had to die too.

He had no idea how far he had run when he reached a wall, the wall that surrounded Glaswell. It was at least two times his height, made from brick, and painted white.

Thankfully there was a tree nearby. Wind climbed it fast and easy. As a cyborg, it was no problem, and it was just as easy to climb over the wall. One swift move and it landed on the other side.

He had to keep running, or at least keep moving. He had great stamina, and it'd keep him on his feet for a while because he didn't dare to stop. Something told him, if he stopped, if he relaxed, his body would give in.

He would die.

He had to keep his system going.

Diane ...

Tears ran down his cheeks. He'd never see her again. He'd never see her smile, her beautiful eyes, or hear her calm voice. The voice he loved so much.

It was over. She was gone.

He'd never imagined it'd feel like his heart was being ripped out of his chest, and all he wanted was to scream, to let the world hear his pain.

Wind ended up in the forest that wasn't far from

Glaswell, despite his inattention to where he'd been going.

His steps slowed, but the pain remained the same. It was as if it was digging a big, black hole inside his chest.

A hole he'd never be able to close.

Celise ...

His beautiful Celise.

He'd abandoned her. He'd run away without looking back, even when she'd called his name. He hadn't been able to stop running. The agony had been too overpowering, blinding him.

It'd all been in vain. Their attempt to save him had brought them nothing. Now Celise would suffer more than she deserved once death took him.

Surrounded by trees, grass, and bushes, he sank to his knees, breathing hard. His heart pounded, but not because of the running.

It was protesting against his bond and trying to keep him alive.

He should've stayed by Celise's side. It would've given him a slight chance of survival. Maybe she could've done something to help him. Out here, nothing could save him.

Weakness filled him.

His limbs had never felt so heavy before. His arms and legs trembled, unable to keep him up. He lost control of them one by one, and to his surprise, it was because of the bond.

It suddenly spread like wildfire in his body, invading his programming, behaving in a way it had never behaved before. Wind had imagined this moment plenty of times. He'd believed he'd just die, that the bond would collapse, but instead, it was functioning as well as always, but in a different way ...

Why was it acting like this? Shouldn't it just stop functioning, like he'd been taught it would, killing him in the process?

Realization hit him as he fell to the ground, unable to keep himself up anymore.

The bond was transforming.

It was turning into a poison that had been lurking in the dark during all these years, waiting for the right moment.

All his life he'd been taught the bond was there to keep the cyborgs alive, that they couldn't exist without it, but he knew better now.

He could live without it.

He felt its true nature now.

It was nothing more but a program meant to keep cyborgs in check, to convince them the bond was as necessary as their next breath. And when their bound one died, it was constructed to make sure they died too.

The Fighters survived because it had failed in its job.

How many cyborgs had had the same realization he

had now just moments before they'd died? Probably many. Most likely every single one, but it'd been too late. None of them had been able to share their discovery before they'd taken their last breath.

And now, it was too late for him as well as darkness slowly took him.

Maybe Nightmare, the leader of the Fighters, wasn't such a fool after all.

CHAPTER 24

"Are you sure he's out here?" Faye looked around the forest with a frown. "All I see is trees."

Celise studied the small laptop in her hands, but it was difficult to focus. She'd never been this afraid before. The stress made her stomach hurt, and she'd almost dropped the computer a few times because of her constant shudders. "My program says he should be here. We need to look around more."

Her friend took a deep breath. "He sure managed to get far during such a short time."

"Cyborgs are faster than humans, and they have better stamina than us."

Faye raised an eyebrow. "Why did MedAct make them better in almost every aspect?"

"You'll have to ask MedAct." The program beeped, indicating a direction Celise followed. She walked by a few trees and bushes, scanning frantically, searching for Wind.

He'd stopped moving. The dot on her screen told her so, and at this moment, she couldn't have been more thankful to herself for creating the program that could locate any cyborg.

She didn't care that other cyborgs probably felt that something was going on in their heads like they'd had when she'd searched for Shade. All she cared about was finding Wind. It had helped Shade find Phoebe through Nightmare when he kidnapped her not long ago, and it would work its magic again. She didn't doubt that.

Frustration filled Celise when she didn't see a glimpse of him. "Come on, Wind. Where are you?" She bit her lip and turned around, perusing the area.

Nothing.

"Damn it." She dried away an irritating tear that ran down her cheek.

Trying to remain calm was becoming difficult. In less than an hour, their lives had turned into chaos.

Diane had died way too soon, and with her, the chance of saving Wind.

Part of her fear was that she didn't know why he'd run away. Was he even still alive? Usually, a cyborg that lost his bound one died within a few minutes, but his eyes had flashed with her.

That kept her hope up.

Celise was grateful for Faye as well. She would've probably completely lost it if it hadn't been for her. Her constant questions had kept her mind on other things as she was trying to find Wind.

"You bonded, right?" Faye asked as she looked around. "Shouldn't that, you know ... like, give him some time or something?"

"It should, but there's no guarantee. One flash is far from enough."

"Will you be able to do something for him?"

She stilled. "I ... don't know." The thought of losing him was unbearable.

Faye laid her hand on her shoulder and smiled. "Whatever happens, I'll stay by your side."

Celise tried to smile back, but it was almost impossible. "Thank you. That means a lot to me."

Her friend glanced over Celise's shoulder. Her jaw dropped, and her eyes widened. "Oh, my God. There he is."

Celise spun around, and the sight of Wind lying on the ground broke her all over again. She ran to him and threw herself on the ground. "Wind!"

His eyes were closed, and his wasn't responding.

Celise checked his pulse. "He's still alive." Relief washed over her, and she could breathe easier.

Faye knelt on the other side of him. "Does that mean he's going to make it?" She studied him with worry.

Celise tore out her scanner from her bag, pulled up Wind's shirt, and pressed the device against his chest as she turned it on. This time, at least, he wasn't going anywhere.

The seconds that followed felt like hours. The results couldn't come fast enough. She looked through it quickly and cringed.

"What does it say?" Faye asked.

Celise frowned. "There's something here I don't understand. The bond still seems to be there, but it's different."

Her friend's eyes widened. "What?"

"It's like ... it has changed character."

"What does that mean?"

Heavy steps rustled in the underbrush as they neared. "It means you're beginning to see the truth."

Celise turned her head when she heard the deep, male voice. Shock went through her as she stared into the shining eyes of Nightmare, the leader of the Fighters.

Faye flew to her feet. "Shit!" She backed two steps, ready to flee.

Celise sat as if paralyzed and stared at the scene taking place in front of her. Three cyborgs had shown up from out of the blue. She hadn't even heard them approach.

Wind had been the only thing on her mind.

Celise had never seen Nightmare in real life, only in media, and the bastard was bigger than she'd imagined. He looked even meaner, with his dark features, wild black hair, and twisted grin. The scar on his throat didn't ease the impression of him.

Neither did the laser gun pointed right at her.

Next to him stood two cyborgs Celise didn't recognize, but they were just as mean-looking as Nightmare. They were tall, muscular, and with cold expressions.

The blond one seemed dead on the inside, no emotions on his face. The look in his eyes was almost robotic.

The redhead, on the other hand, sent cold shivers down her spine. He radiated rage in a way that neither Nightmare nor the blond cyborg did. She'd never seen so much hate in someone's eyes before.

"I must say I didn't expect to find anyone but the cyborg here," Nightmare said. He looked at Faye. "But it's nice to see you again, Faye. Silver can't wait to see you."

Faye took another step back, worry in her eyes. "We should leave, Celise. Like right now."

Determination awakened within Celise. She wouldn't let these cyborgs scare her. "I'm not leaving Wind." She glared at Nightmare. "Why are *you* here?"

The rogue leader studied her and the device she held, ignoring her question. "You're one of MedAct's doctors."

It was a statement.

She frowned. "I work for them, yes."

He rubbed his chin and exchanged a look with the other Fighters.

A feeling of dread went through her when the redhead grinned.

The blond only nodded.

It was as if they had a conversation without words, but cyborgs couldn't communicate telepathically, so they had to know something *she* didn't.

"You can't save him, you know," Nightmare said.

Anger awakened within her. "Watch me." Celise ignored him and focused on Wind. She pressed the scanner against his chest again. She didn't have time for anything else. Her cyborg's life hung on a thin thread, and if she didn't do something soon, he'd die.

The scanning indicated the bond wasn't working as it should. Probably because of Diane's death, but something also told her that wasn't only it.

The bond shouldn't be there in the first place. It should've malfunctioned as soon as Wind had spotted Diane's body, but the bond didn't show any signs of malfunctioning. Instead, it was as powerful as ever.

She'd never seen what actually happened when a cyborg died. She only knew the theory, and what the scan said went against everything she'd been taught about the bond.

Nightmare handed the gun to the redheaded cyborg and crouched next to her. "Your name is Celise?"

She only nodded, not taking her eyes off of the scanner.

"You know who I am?"

Celise frowned. "Is there someone who doesn't?"

"I guess you're right, but you don't seem afraid."

Faye snorted. "She just hasn't had the pleasure of seeing your exquisite personality for herself yet."

Nightmare glared at Faye. "But you have, and I'm sure I left an impression on you, just as *you* left an impression on Silver." He turned his gaze back to Celise. "How long have you been working for MedAct?"

"About six years. Why do you care?"

He once again avoided her question. "What does the scan tell you?"

Suspicion washed over her. "Why should I tell you?"

"Let me guess. It tells you the bond is still there, and that it's fully functioning, but its behavior has changed. It's not doing what it was designed for anymore. It is instead spreading in his body, shutting off one part after another."

Celise stared, tried not to show her surprise. "How do you know that?"

He frowned, ignoring her question a third time. "But I must say I'm surprised it's taking this long." Nightmare ripped the scanner from her hands, making her wince. "He should be dead by now."

Silence filled the area as the leader studied the scan. Then he lowered the device and gave her a look that made her tense. It told her he was someone she shouldn't take lightly. He was dangerous. He'd snap her neck without a second thought, but there was also something else.

Loneliness.

So much loneliness ...

For a second, it made her feel sorry for him, but then she remembered *who* he was. Celise grabbed Wind's hand in a hopeless attempt to protect him from the Fighters leader.

He wanted something. That was why he was there, but how had he found them? "There's another bond here," Nightmare said. His eyes narrowed as he looked at her hand holding Wind's. "You were trying to take over his bond, weren't you?"

It really was scary how observant he was. She took a deep breath and tried to remain calm. "I don't have time for this. I need to get him to MedAct so I can save him."

He frowned again. "You haven't told Jade yet?"

"There was no time." Celise couldn't believe she was telling him all this, but despite the unnerving look in his eyes, there was also something else there.

Understanding.

What the hell was going on? How could he possibly know these things?

She narrowed her eyes. "You've seen this before."

A grin spread on his plum lips. It made him look handsome and harmless. Almost. "Oh, yes. Many times."

"Tell me what's going on?"

He got to his feet. "Come with me, and I'll *show* you."

Celise's jaw dropped. "What?"

Faye gasped. She didn't say anything, but the fear in her eyes was unmistakable.

"You really expect me to go with you? I need to take Wind to MedAct. I can't do anything for him here. My bond to him is the only thing keeping him alive. The scan tells me I have less than two hours to save him."

His face went expressionless. "MedAct can't do anything for him, and trust me, they *won't*. The bond has already made the transformation. To them, he's already dead."

This jerk was starting to get on her nerves. "What do you mean? They always do everything in their power to save a cyborg."

Nightmare sighed. "You've been working for them for six years, and yet, you know so little." Without warning, he grabbed her hand and pulled her to her feet. "I'm willing to give you a chance of a lifetime, Celise— the insight of the Fighters' lives. I can bring you inside our headquarters, show you our world."

She blinked. Everything inside her told her not to trust

this cyborg. She'd heard enough about him to know he was the last person she should trust, but at the same time, there was something off with Wind's bond, and *he* seemed to have the answer.

"Why?" she asked.

"Because I can show you the truth MedAct doesn't want you to see." He gave her a once-over. "It's obvious you're not one of their top doctors, and because of that, I'm willing to show you what no one on the outside has ever seen. They've barely let you inside MedAct's facility, have they? You seem ... fresh." He grinned.

"Don't do it, Celise." Faye gave her a wary look.

She shook her head, emotions going wild inside her. "You don't even know me."

"No, I don't, but I know your kind. I can save him, and it's obvious you care about him. Besides, I've had my eyes on him since we met some time ago," Nightmare answered.

Celise gawked. "You've been watching him?"

Nightmare shrugged. "It's not difficult to bug someone, especially a cyborg who's too distressed to notice. I saw him as a potential candidate for my tests, but I guess that's not going to happen now. He's in no condition for what I had in mind for him. You on the other hand; you're exactly what I need."

She took a step back. "What do you mean?"

"I need someone on the inside." He crossed his arms

over his chest. "You've just seen what no MedAct doctor in your position has seen. You've stumbled upon something you don't understand, and you want answers." He pointed at Wind. "You have your proof lying right in front of you. The scan doesn't lie. You know that. Come with me, and I'll tell you everything."

Celise swallowed and licked her lips. "There's something wrong with the bond."

He nodded. "Yes, and no. The bond is functioning just as it was designed to. It's just that few know what it really is designed for."

"And that is?"

He reached out his hand. "Come with me, and I'll show you."

"Celise ..." Faye warned.

Nightmare turned to her. "Don't worry, Faye. You're coming with us, too."

Her eyes widened. "In your dreams!"

"You have to finish what you started, my dear, or Silver will die." He turned back to Celise. "How will it be?"

Faye glared at the leader. "I thought you were against the bond. I remember you said it isn't real."

"It isn't real, but you got it me all wrong."

She snorted. "I was there when you hurt Shade, so don't take me for a fool."

"I'll prove you wrong." The light in his shining eyes intensified.

"You expect me to just trust you?" Celise asked. "You must be a fool if you think I'll do that, but I guess you won't give me a choice."

His face turned serious. "I *will* give you a choice, Celise, to show you I'm not the man you think I am. Come with me, and I'll tell you everything, but if you refuse, I'll let you go. You can take Wind to MedAct, and watch him die. They'll tell you there's nothing they can do to save him. I can assure you that."

"Don't trust him, Celise!" Faye yelled. "He almost killed Shade."

"To save many, a few must be sacrificed," he said, giving Faye a cold look.

Celise's gaze lingered between Faye and Nightmare. "What if I go with you? What happens then? Will I be able to leave?"

"I doubt you'll want to leave once I've shown you the truth." The leader placed his hand on his chest. "But I swear on my honor, no harm will come to you, Wind, or Faye. I'm willing to trust you enough to even show you where our headquarter is. I'm putting the Fighters' fate in your hands, and if you still don't believe me after you've heard me out, you can go to MedAct and tell them all about it."

Celise couldn't believe this was happening. Was he really willing to trust *her*? Just like that? He was either a fool or desperate.

Her gaze wandered to Wind. He still hadn't moved. His eyes were closed as he lay still on the ground. He seemed peaceful, but with each minute, he came closer and closer to death.

Her heart bled. It cried from the knowledge that she'd lose him if she didn't do something.

She didn't know what the right thing to do was, but she'd seen a glimpse of something that shouldn't be there. It was something MedAct had never even mentioned, and *that* awakened her suspicion.

Something was off ...

Very off ...

She took a deep breath. "I'll probably regret this, but I'll go with you, under the conditions you mentioned. No harm shall come to me, Faye, or Wind, and we'll be able to leave whenever we like."

Nightmare nodded. "You have my word."

Faye didn't seem happy but didn't object. She looked at Celise. "I promised I'd stay by your side, no matter what happened, and that's what I'll do." She threw up her arms and sighed. "Here we go again."

CHAPTER 25

The van sped down the road. The blond cyborg drove it, and no one spoke. The only sound that was heard was the tires against the pavement.

The vehicle was big enough to accommodate ten people, but apart from the front seats for the driver and a passenger, the windowless rear only had seats for four.

It surprised Celise that it was clean and seemed well taken care of. The interior was white, and black rubber mats covered the floor. Guns hung behind the driver, locked behind bars, and next to it, a med kit. There was even a computer tablet attached there. She had, for some reason, imagined the Fighters to be a sloppy gang, but much pointed to the opposite.

Nightmare and the red-haired cyborg sat in the back with her and Faye.

Wind lay on the floor with the scanner against his

chest. If anything changed, she'd know instantly.

The worry refused to release her, making her keep a watchful eye on him. She could only hope their destination wasn't far.

Celise looked at Faye, sitting next to her, but her friend didn't spare her a glance. Faye was being so mellow. Why? There was no trace of the rebellious person she usually was.

She had suspicions to why Faye had agreed to this. She'd seen the guilt in Faye's eyes when Nightmare had mentioned Silver. Maybe, she had finally accepted she had to face him.

Celise turned her gaze to the redheaded cyborg. He had unusual beauty and appearance, with high cheekbones and a wide mouth. She hadn't paid much attention to him before, but she did now, and his shining eyes had a red glow. She'd never seen that before. She'd also never seen such pale skin. It was almost as if he lacked pigmentation.

"I'm Blaze," he suddenly said.

She winced. Hadn't expected him to speak, considering the anger she'd seen in his eyes in the forest. Strangely, that rage didn't seem to be there anymore. Instead, his eyes were filled with anticipation.

"I'd say it's nice to meet you, Blaze, but I don't think it fits the situation."

His lips twitched. "Don't worry. You have nothing to

fear from me. We've been waiting for you."

She blinked. "What?"

Blaze looked at Nightmare with a silent question in his eyes.

The rogue leader only nodded, and the redhead turned back to Celise. "The world has a messed-up image about us. Most people believe we're crazy, dangerous, and not reliable."

Celise frowned. "You kill people."

Blaze remained calm. "Not without cause."

"And you rob places."

"Also, not without cause. We have to survive."

"Many of you are also damaged because of the broken bond."

He nodded. "We're damaged because the bond tried to kill us once our bound one died. We do everything we can for those cyborgs. No one is terminated unless there's no other way."

"So I'd say the world has a rather good image of you."

His lips tensed, but he still remained calm. "There's more to us than you think. You'd be dead by now if we were the bad guys media portray us to be. We're about to show you everything about us, and we'll even let you go once our talk is over. We're sacrificing everything here. Doesn't that mean anything?"

Silence filled the van for a short while.

"You need someone to tell your story," Celise gasped.

Blaze nodded again. "We've been looking for the right person for years, and it couldn't be just anybody. It had to be a doctor who works for MedAct. We've had our eyes on you, and other doctors, but *you* are the one we considered."

Her jaw dropped, and she stared at the cyborg as everything he'd said sank in. "Why me?"

"Because you seemed like a kind and understanding person. You also have something most of the other doctors lack."

"And what is that?"

"You see us as equals, and you really care about us." A gentle smile played on his lips as he reclined against the wall of the van. "You're also the one who created the program that can track cyborgs using the forgotten signal inside our programming."

Shock went through her, and she straightened her shoulders. "How did you know that?"

His smile slid into a grin before he chuckled.

Nightmare chuckled with him.

"I didn't," Blaze said. "*You* just confirmed our suspicions."

Her heart pounded as she stared at them. They seemed amused by her surprise. Celise was unable to speak. Her brain felt like toast, but as she slowly came back to her senses, she understood it'd been just a matter of time before they'd find out.

"We might be a bunch of damaged cyborgs, but we're still smart," Nightmare said. "We managed to track the signal you sent out. When we realized it came from Glaswell, it didn't take much to understand that one of the doctors who work for MedAct operates it from there."

Defeat filled her. "Is my program the reason I'm here?"

"No. We've already told you why you're here. You're here because we need you. We want you to see the truth. We want you to understand everything." The leader's eyes were serious.

She nodded, relief flooding her. For a short moment there, she'd thought she'd been played.

Celise glanced at Faye. She'd remained silent during the whole conversation. It worried her since it was so unusual for her friend. She took a deep breath. "Why do you trust me? It's obvious you'd been spying on me, but you don't *know* me."

"We don't trust you," Nightmare said, "but we're willing to take our chances. Something has to be done to change our fate. We hope you're one step in the right direction."

"And what is your goal?"

The cyborgs remained silent for a while. They exchanged glances as if they were trying to decide what to admit. "To eliminate the bond and take down MedAct,"

Blaze finally said.

Faye snorted, breaking her silence. "Good luck with that."

Nightmare snorted. "I know you both think it sounds crazy, but when you know what *we* know, you'll rethink."

The van slowed, and a few seconds later, turned right. The ground changed and became bumpier.

Celise tried to look through the driver's window. She had no idea where they were, and all she saw were trees. It'd taken about fifteen minutes to get from where they'd been.

"Where are we?" Faye asked.

"About an hour from Glaswell," Blaze answered.

The vehicle drove for another minute before coming to a halt.

Nightmare opened the back door and got out. Faye followed, and Blaze after her.

Celise hesitated. She looked at Wind, who still lay on the floor with closed eyes. The scanner on his chest still indicated the same thing — he was dying, and if she didn't stop it soon, there'd be no way to bring him back.

His bond to Diane had changed. It should be gone, but instead, it was still there, and she had no idea how to interpret that. She just hoped Nightmare had a solution.

"Don't worry," Blaze said. "Heaven will carry him inside."

Celise frowned. "Heaven?"

"The bastard who drove us here."

The driver's door opened, and seconds later, the blond cyborg came to the back of the van.

His emotionless dead eyes made her jump. He seemed so different from the calm Blaze. It was as if there just wasn't anything on the inside. Usually, people showed some kind of emotion, but when it came to Heaven, there was nothing.

Nothing at all.

As if he was empty.

"Relax," Blaze said, offering her his hand. "Heaven won't harm Wind."

Heaven's dead eyes looked at her. "Hurting Wind is not a logical action. We need you. Therefore, he cannot be harmed."

Celise blinked, unable to move. Her instincts told her to stay put, to not leave Wind, in case he'd need her. Plus, she'd have to remove the scanner from his chest in order for Heaven to carry him.

The emotionless cyborg was just as attractive as Blaze with his androgynous features. He was tall and muscular, and she didn't doubt he was strong enough to carry Wind.

With a heavy heart, Celise grabbed the scanner and stepped out from the van. She was doing the right thing, wasn't she?

Celise couldn't recall how many times she'd changed her mind during the journey. She should've gone to MedAct instead. What could Nightmare possibly do to save Wind, anyway? She doubted he had the necessary expertise and equipment.

Celise scanned their surroundings. The car was parked on a slim gravel road. Where it continued, she had no idea. A beautiful forest with healthy trees and tall grass encircled them. Probably the same forest from before, since it stretched on for miles. "Is this where you live?"

"You could say that," Nightmare said as Heaven lifted out Wind from the back of the van.

Faye frowned. "There's nothing but trees here. Are you guys some kind of Robin Hood type?"

His lips didn't even twitch. "I guess you'll find out soon." The leader walked into the forest, approaching a small clearing. He stopped in front of a tree and placed his hand against its trunk. A blue light came from underneath his hand just before a clicking sound was heard.

Celise gasped when the ground started to tremor.

"Shit!" Faye yelled, taking a step back. "What's going on?"

"You're about to enter our home," Blaze said with a smile.

Something seemed to be approaching from underground judging by the sound. It became louder and louder, and before Celise could fully grasp what the sound was, an elevator rose from the ground with grass still attached to the top. It came up from the middle of the small, but open area. The elevator had no walls, just glass surrounded it.

Amazement filled her. She'd never expected this.

Most people believed the Fighters lived shabby and dirty lives, constantly on the run from MedAct and the police, but *this* indicated something completely different.

It almost excited her to find out where the elevator went. A tiny glimpse of hope awakened within her as well. Maybe there *was* a chance to save Wind here after all.

"You expect me to get inside that?" Faye asked with huge eyes.

"Yes," Nightmare answered.

"Well, forget it! You won't trick me into doing such a stupid thing. Who knows what's down there!"

Heaven seemed uninterested in the sudden fuss. Instead, he entered the elevator with Wind in his arms. He stared ahead, waiting.

Celise's legs moved of their own accord toward the elevator. She had to go with Wind, no matter what. She was the only one who could defend him if anything went wrong.

He was so helpless right now, and she'd give up her life to protect his if she had to. She didn't trust the Fighters, but hope had brought her here.

Maybe there was more to them, after all.

Heaven spared her a glance when she entered the elevator.

"Celise! You can't be serious," Faye said.

"I can't leave him. I just can't."

Disbelief colored her friend's features, but Celise avoided reminding her about her promise to stay no matter what. She couldn't demand that of Faye. The fear in her eyes was obvious, and the decision had to be hers.

Celise preferred to have Faye by her side. It kept her somewhat grounded, and who knew what would happen once the elevator reached its destination. Worst case, she'd lose it and break down if her hope had been in vain.

The Fighters didn't say anything.

Instead, they entered the elevator as well.

Faye cursed and stomped with her left foot. She pressed her lips together and fisted her hands, glaring at the Fighters. "I'm sure I'll regret this, but fine. I'll go." She stepped onto the elevator, pointing a threatening finger at them. "But if any of you as much as touches me, Wind, or Celise the wrong way, I will hit you where it hurts the most."

Nightmare only grinned and pressed a digital button on the glass wall.

Celise tensed when the elevator started to move down. She closed her eyes and prayed she'd done the right thing.

CHAPTER 26

The elevator seemed to go forever. They were surrounded by nothing but metal beyond the glass walls, creating a claustrophobic sensation in Celise's gut.

Nightmare seemed pleased with himself, and that worried her because she had no idea what he could be thinking.

Blaze seemed to have a watchful eye on Wind. He scanned him over and over again with his gaze. He smiled when he noticed her watching him. "I'm the medic here. I used to work at a human hospital near MedAct with my bound one before she died. My specialty is humans. Yours is cyborgs. We will complement each other well."

Celise gave him a gentle smile back. For some reason, she was starting to like this Fighter, despite the hatred she'd seen in his eyes at first. "You haven't worked with cyborgs?" she asked.

"Not until I came here. I've learned a lot over the past three years I've been here, but it's a little like asking a veterinarian to perform an operation on a human."

She nodded. "I understand, but you don't like MedAct's doctors, do you?"

His smile faded. "Why do you ask?"

"The way you looked at me when you first saw me ..."

He took a deep breath, looking away. "It's a long story, but maybe I'll tell you one day."

"I'm looking forward to hearing it." Celise couldn't help but feel she and Blaze had gotten closer these past few minutes. He actually made her feel safer, as if she'd made the right decision.

"What happened to your bound one?" Faye asked.

The elevator slowed, and a second later, it stopped. The doors opened, and a long, wide windowless corridor with white walls and ceiling lamps greeted them. It looked clinical and fresh.

A slightly chilly and sterile scent filled Celise's nose.

Nightmare and Heaven stepped off the elevator. Celise followed, but Blaze and Faye remained.

Blaze looked at Faye. His gaze was cold, but it wasn't directed at her. He seemed to be pondering if he should answer her or not. Finally, he relaxed and turned toward the corridor. "MedAct killed her," he said and left the elevator.

218

And just like that, the conversation was over as he hurried out.

Celise quickened her step but didn't say anything. His statement was like a blow to the stomach. She wanted to ask him what had happened, but she doubted he'd answer. It couldn't be true, could it?

Faye joined her. "I guess I shouldn't have asked."

She gave her a smile and opened her mouth to tell her friend not to worry about it, but a sudden noise drew her attention.

Talking men.

There was an open door right in front of them. It was wide and seemed to lead into a big room. She slowed her steps.

Faye followed her lead.

"Don't worry," Blaze said, noticing their distress. "They won't hurt you. They've been waiting for you as well."

Celise took a deep breath. She had no idea how many Fighters were in there, but it sounded like plenty.

Faye seemed just as tense as she was.

Wind, on the other hand, still wasn't moving. The two hours would come to an end soon, and she still had no idea what was wrong with him.

Or if she could save him.

The room was huge; some kind of gathering room. There were three sofas, a pool table, a television, and tables with computers, along with other entertainment equipment. It was windowless and lacked decorations, but it looked clean and smelled fresh.

Her gaze swept the area. She'd expected to see about five Fighters, but there were a lot more of them.

A lot more.

She counted at least twenty, and they came in all shapes and sizes, but it was obvious they were all cyborgs, judging by their shining eyes.

The whole room came to a halt as they entered. Sitting Fighters stood and stared, with dropped jaws. Someone dropped a book that hit the floor with a loud thud.

Celise's heart pounded like never before. Fear skittered down her spine, and she fought shudders. Anything could happen. Her life, but especially, Wind's life could be in danger.

Without a second thought, she shifted closer to Heaven and touched Wind's arm.

Heaven didn't pay her any attention, but she was grateful he didn't drop her cyborg. He had to be heavy, but cyborgs were a lot stronger than humans.

A long silence filled the room, and it ratcheted up her stress. Every minute counted for Wind, but something told her, they had to go through this room to get to wherever they were heading.

One of the Fighters approached. He wasn't as tall as the

others, but he was attractive with big eyes, and long dark hair. "What's going on? Who are they?"

A few other Fighters moved closer. It was obvious not all of them were well. The exhaustion and pain in their eyes was unmistakable. It awakened Celise's instincts as a doctor. It made her want to help each and every one of them.

Nightmare only halted for a few seconds before he continued through the room toward another door. "I brought the MedAct doctor I talked about, along with Silver's bound one, but we don't have time to talk. Save your questions for later. We have a cyborg to save." He ignored the others who tried to approach and exited through the other door.

"I am *not* his bound one," Faye mumbled in an angry tone.

They exited the huge room and entered a new hallway. Celise had no idea where the leader was taking them, but it was like walking in a labyrinth. They took many different turns, and there were no signs, but Nightmare seemed sure about where he was going.

"What is this place?" Faye asked. "It almost feels like we're inside a hospital."

"It's an abandoned bunker from a war a long time ago," Nightmare answered. "I found it over thirty years ago and turned it into our home. It was a filthy and uncomfortable place back then, but we've worked hard to make it livable."

"I see that. Everything is so sterile and white. I never expected that of a bunch like you."

Nightmare gave Faye the evil glare but didn't stop walking. "I feel sorry for Silver, who'll have to put up with you for the rest of his life."

Faye bristled and made tight fists as she scowled. She opened her mouth to say something, but Celise grabbed her arm.

"Whatever you were going to say, don't," she whispered.

Nightmare stopped in front of double doors. He placed his hand on a scan plate next to the doors. A second later, they opened.

Celise recognized medical equipment as they went in. There was everything from stethoscopes to big machines.

The room itself was wide, and bright with white walls. It even seemed more sterile then the rest of the place, if that was even possible. She couldn't help but smile as it made her feel like home.

There were three hospital beds, two cabinets filled with medicine, needles, and other necessities that stood near the doors. Two other cabinets contained towels, wash clothes, and beddings. There were even two laptops in the room, lying on the desk that stood against one of the walls.

"Wow," Faye said. "You sure are prepared for anything."

Heaven put Wind on one of the beds. "I'll go and

hide the van while you take care of him." He left without another word.

Blaze got to work as Nightmare sat down by one of the computers. The medic cyborg pulled a big machine consisting of a large screen and cords closer to the bed and shoved Wind's shirt up. He started to attach the cords to his chest and head.

The machine came on by itself.

Celise's assumption it was to monitor his vitals was corrected when she read on, "ready to transmit" on its screen. It was some sort of electric charger.

Worry hit her chest, and she rushed to the side of the bed. "What are you doing?"

Blaze didn't look up; he kept attaching the chords to Wind. "We're saving him."

"What does that mean, exactly? I thought we were going to fix the bond."

"There's nothing wrong with the bond. It's doing exactly what it was designed to do. You saw it yourself."

"It was doing something, but I have no idea what."

He stilled and looked her deep in the eyes. His understanding and kind gaze made her wince. She'd never expected to see such kind eyes on a Fighter, especially one who'd shown nothing but anger at first. She swallowed as nervousness swept over her.

"I'm trying to stop the bond from killing Wind.

Unfortunately, when the bond realizes it won't succeed with its mission, it'll start screaming after a new bound one. Luckily for Wind, he already has a new bond initiated, so when his old one realizes it can't kill him, it'll let the new bond take over."

His words made Celise's heart race. "*How* exactly?"

"Through the machine, I'll transmit a signal into his bond and block it from doing any more harm," Nightmare said, punching keys on the laptop. "Trust me, it'll work. It's never failed."

"What kind of signal?" Her hands shook.

"I created it myself many years ago. It's saved every cyborg I've transmitted it into. It's in my system as well. I don't like using it, but I prefer to have it instead of needing it, and not having it."

Hesitation hit her. "I want to see it."

"Time's ticking, Celise. You can examine the signal and anything you want ... but later." He kept pushing the keys.

She clenched her fists, unsure of what do to. Time wasn't on their side, but Celise didn't trust Nightmare, either. For all she knew, he could be transmitting anything he wanted into Wind, and she wouldn't be able to tell what he'd done before it was too late.

"As soon as the signal is transmitted, an electric shock will go through his system," Blaze said. "It won't be painful, but it'll start waking him up. It'll take some time before his

224

body responds, but he'll be able to hear us, and you'll have to play along."

She blinked. "Play along?"

"The sooner his instincts awaken, the better."

Nightmare approached the bed. "The stronger his need to defend you from us is, the stronger defense the signal will give him."

Celise frowned.

What?

Faye grinned. She seemed to understand what the Fighters were talking about. "This sounds like a lot of fun." She sat on one of the other beds. "I'll watch from here."

That only confused her even more. "*What* are you talking about?"

The rogue leader grinned too. "You'll see, but don't worry, as soon as he's up on his feet, we'll leave you two alone for a few hours so you can bond."

Realization hit her, but she was too stunned to say anything. They were about to tease Wind in the worst way they could tease a cyborg. The Fighters were going to make him believe they wanted to take her away from him.

Blaze watched the machine's screen. Beeping sounds came from it, and a green button lit up in one corner. "It's ready."

Nightmare backed away. "Everyone, keep your distance to Celise. He'll be very angry once he's up on his feet." He grabbed Faye's arm and pulled her closer to the door.

She didn't object.

"Celise, you stay where you are," the leader ordered.

Blaze took a deep breath. "Let's begin." He pushed a button.

CHAPTER 27

Darkness was all around him. He was floating in a big, black nothing, where silence ruled. Peacefulness made him feel safe, filling him with a sense of freedom.

Maybe this was how it felt like to be dead.

Wind had no idea how long he'd been here, but he didn't care. He liked the sensations and didn't want to leave. He needed the calmness because he had a feeling something bad had happened just before he'd come here.

Something he didn't want to remember.

"Is he awake?"

Wind tensed as a male voice penetrated the void. He didn't recognize the voice, but at the same time, couldn't get away from the feeling he'd heard it somewhere before.

"He's awake," another male voice answered. This one was unfamiliar.

"Good. How's the signal doing?"

Sounds of movement reached his ears, and he suddenly felt he was lying on something soft. The darkness slowly slipped away. He wasn't dead after all. He was very much alive, but couldn't move. His body felt like a sack of bricks, and his muscles ached all over. It made him groan, but no sound would leave his lips.

"The signal is working," the unknown man said. "Within a few minutes, his old bond will be blocked for good. It won't be able to hurt him anymore, and he'll be able to move once the signal is in place."

What were they talking about? What signal?

He scanned his body, trying to detect if something was off, but he couldn't feel anything wrong.

"Is he going to be all right?"

Celise!

Joy filled his heart. He wanted to smile, but his body didn't respond. He wanted so badly to open his eyes and look at her.

"Yes, don't worry, sweetie," the familiar male voice said. "He'll do just fine."

Sweetie?

Wind wanted to fist his hands, but again, his body wouldn't obey.

"Is he in pain?" she asked.

"No," the familiar voice answered. "This signal is completely harmless. He won't feel it working. He'll only feel the result."

The familiar male's words weren't comforting.

What kind of result was he talking about?

"Good," Celise said and took an audible deep breath.

There was worry in her voice. Wind wished he could hold her, tell her everything was going to be all right. He felt fine, apart from the muscle ache. It was as if nothing had happened.

He stilled.

Had something happened?

He searched his memory. As a cyborg, he should be able to remember *everything*, but his mind was blank. What was going on? Where was he, and how had they ended up wherever they were?

Wind focused. He had to put more effort into it. It was important he remembered.

The unknown male had mentioned something about his old bond.

He felt a gentle pressure on his arms.

"I'm right here, Wind."

Celise.

Her sweet voice filled his starving heart.

She caressed his cheek. The touch made him tingle all over from need. "You'd never believe me if I told you where we are, but when you open your eyes, remember you're safe. We all are."

He sensed her walk away, and he missed her touch. He needed it so much!

Wind tried to move, but his muscles didn't respond. Frustration washed over him.

"You shouldn't be that close to him, sweetie," the familiar voice said. "He'll gain movement back fast. He might accidently hurt you then."

Wind cringed on the inside.

Why did that man call Celise sweetie again?

"Come here," the man went on. "I can hold you and protect you. My arms are strong and safe. My body is warm and cozy. I ensure you that."

What the?!

Wind wanted to scream. Who did he think he was? If the stranger touched his bound one, he'd make sure the man would regret it for the rest of his life.

Bound one ...

He gasped when an image of a blonde beauty, smiling at him, crossed his mind.

Diane.

His bound one.

A new image filled his mind. She lay still in his arms on the floor. Her body was cold, and she wasn't breathing. The gut-wrenching agony he'd felt then filled him once again, but he was unable to scream.

He'd lost her, but somehow, he was still alive.

His arms moved.

A sigh came from the other man; the voice he didn't recognize. "Don't listen to him, Celise. I'm maybe not as big and dark as that bastard, but my embrace is much more loving and caring." The man chuckled.

"Um ..."

Celise.

There was hesitation in her voice.

Something clicked in Wind's mind.

Big, dark bastard.

That voice.

Why did all of that sound so familiar?

A female giggled.

Faye.

She was here, too?

"Aren't you excited, Celise? I wouldn't mind this much attention myself. Especially not from these two hot Fighters."

Fighters?

Somehow, Wind managed to tense his body, fist his knuckles, and give a roar of anger.

Fighters!

It meant the males in the room with Faye and Celise were two unbound cyborgs.

He recognized the voice now. It belonged to Nightmare! How could Celise claim they were safe if he was in the room with them?

Nightmare sighed. "Nice going, Faye."

"What?"

"You just had to tell him we're Fighters," the other male said.

Why on earth were they trying to take Celise away from him?

Somehow, they seemed to know his bond to Diane was damaged. It'd changed before he'd passed out in the forest.

They'd brought him somewhere, imprisoned both Faye and Celise, and somehow brainwashed them.

Well, at least brainwashed Faye.

Or maybe not.

Faye was Faye after all.

They'd said something about a signal. They'd done something to him! Had they transferred the same signal into him that had almost killed Shade?

Pure fury filled every pore of his body and exploded.

Wind opened his eyes and sat up at the speed of light. His gaze locked at the four pair of eyes staring back at him. He recognized Nightmare. The Fighter stood by the double doors next to Faye, and a cyborg with red hair he hadn't seen before.

He scanned the room. They were in a bright, and sterile-looking medical room. Was he at MedAct? No, he couldn't be. Nightmare would never set his foot in MedAct.

Celise moved closer to his bed.

Wind grabbed her arm, pulling her into his body, but he didn't look away from the Fighters. Instead, he kept scowling at them, warning them not to come any closer.

"I guess it's time for us to leave," the redheaded Fighter said before he turned to the door. "Good luck, Celise."

The unfamiliar cyborg, Nightmare, and Faye fled the room.

Wind didn't miss the wide grin on Faye's lips as the doors locked behind them.

Irritation burned as he glanced at Celise. "What's going on?" He looked around again. "Where am I?"

She placed her arms on his shoulders, as if to calm him. "How do you feel?"

He frowned. His instinct to defend her didn't ease, neither did his anger or his desire for her. "Strangely enough, I feel fine. Why aren't I dead?"

Her smile was tremulous. "Your bond to me gave us enough time to save you, but honestly, I didn't do a thing. Nightmare and Blaze saved you."

That didn't make any sense, but with each passing second, it was becoming more and more difficult to focus on anything else but Celise. She looked so beautiful, even if her clothes were dirty, smudged with grass and mud. Her blonde hair needed a brush, and her eyes told him how tired she was.

What had she been through while he'd been unconscious?

Something had definitely been done to him. His bond to Diane was still there, but its progress had been stopped. Instead, his initiated bond to Celise was taking over.

And it was taking over fast.

At first, it was like a frustrated whimper inside him, but it didn't take long before the negative emotions melted into a desperate cry.

The bond wanted one thing.

One thing only ...

Celise.

It suddenly became hotter in the room. A thin coat of sweat broke out on his skin, an ache of need awakened in his gut. It made him groan and shift on the bed. His desire grew as his cock strained against his pants. Wind swallowed and clenched his fists. "You can explain everything to me later. My bond to you is all of a sudden going crazy. It feels like I'll die if I don't have you within the next minute."

Celise's smile turned into a grin.

He snorted as he stood from the bed, shoving his pants off. "It's not funny. I'm so hard I'm going to burst."

She looked down, and her cute cheeks shone pink. "I can see that."

"Don't toy with me, Celise. I can't handle it right now."

Impatiently, he tugged her into an embrace. He pressed his lips to hers with a need so great it made his head spin.

What he'd experienced with her during the first flash was nothing compared to now. Her nearness, the warmth of her skin, the tender sounds she made as he kissed her, her raspy breathing as he explored her body with determined caresses, it all sparked a fierce fire inside him.

His bond to her had to be sealed now that his bond to Diane was fading. He had no choice in the matter. It became his one and only mission. They needed two more flashes, and something told him they'd get them, right here, right now.

Wind wouldn't, couldn't, stop until it happened.

He showered her with lustful kisses and starving touches as he stripped one piece of clothing after another from her.

It made her giggle, and she covered herself with her arms when her breasts sprung free as he stripped her off of the bra.

He found it cute that she was still shy in front of him, despite all the things they'd already shared.

Wind grinned.

It was time to take her to a completely new level.

He laid her naked on the bed, with her legs still on the floor. He enjoyed the aroused look in her eyes and the flush on her cheeks.

She watched him with curiosity, obviously wondering what he'd do next.

He was about to surprise her.

Wind leaned over her, slowly sliding his hands over her small body. She was tiny compared to him. Celise barely reached his shoulders, and that just made him want to protect her even more.

There were Fighters beyond these walls, but not even they could stop him from bonding with her. He was even unable to stop himself.

She moaned and closed her eyes as he explored her body.

He teased her nipples with his mouth and fingers. It pleased him to see how she reacted to the pleasure he enwrapped her in. Wind hungered for her like never before. The feel of her bare and warm body against his was like an aphrodisiac. He'd wanted to take her to a new level, but it seemed like *she* was taking him there, as her hands slid through his thick hair.

He traveled lower with his kisses, reaching her navel, and still continuing lower, leaving light brushes with his lips on her pelvis.

Her body tensed and a gasp left her mouth.

He raised his gaze and met her surprised stare.

"What are you doing?" she asked.

Wind gave her a wicked grin. "Exactly what I want to do."

She jerked when he licked her sensitive lips. "I don't ... think I'm ready for that."

He chuckled. The anticipation in her eyes was unmistakable. "Oh, I think you are." He leaned down again, parting her legs to get better access. "Just relax and enjoy."

Celise trembled. "Wind, I ... Oh!"

Wind didn't give her time to think too much. Instead, he gave her everything at once. Despite their night together, this was the first time he'd touched her this way. Getting that shyness out of her was a process, and he looked forward to it.

A whimper left her lips as he licked and nipped her aroused clit. One touch was enough, and she was lost in the world of pleasure as he explored her with a starved frenzy.

He couldn't help it. His body was on fire, his need greater than before. Hearing her moans, feeling her quiver under him as he kept her locked in place only triggered him to keep going. The way Celise moved her hips against his tongue made him almost lose his mind.

Her breathing became harsher, and she hugged the linens desperately.

She was close so Wind increased the pressure. Seconds later, her cry of pleasure filled the room. He didn't ease up. Instead, he took her through the intense orgasm for as long as she could take it, gripping her firmer in his arms as her limbs shook. Not until she grabbed his head and pushed him away did he stop.

He dried his mouth and grinned, leaning over her.

A satisfied smile decorated her features. She looked so beautiful with her after-sex look.

"That was amazing," Celise whispered. Her cheeks were flushed.

"We're not done yet." He dipped down to kiss her, but a sudden warm feeling in his eyes made him halt. The heat intensified and it took him only a second to understand what was going on. He turned his head away from her just in time as his eyes flashed.

The change inside him was instant.

His bond had accepted her.

All they needed now was the last flash that would seal it.

As he met her gaze again, Wind felt his love for her grow inside his heart. He'd die without her now.

Her eyes were wide as she stared at him, then she relaxed into a smile. "I never actually dared to imagine we'd reach this point."

"Why?"

"I guess it still feels kind of unreal. You and me, *together*. Just last week that was a dream that would never come true. And yet, here we are."

He kissed her cheek, slowly entering her and earning a moan. "You're stuck with me now." Wind moved closer to her ear. "Promise me one thing, Celise," he whispered as she wrapped her legs around him.

Passion returned to her face as he slowly built up a rhythm.

"Anything."

"Promise, when your time to die comes, you'll let me die with you."

She tensed underneath him. "Are you sure you want that?"

Wind nodded. "I won't be able to handle a third bound one."

Celise remained silent for a while, but the answer was written in her eyes. She wanted him to live, just like Diane had wanted him to live.

He was here because of her wish. He'd respected it, but deep down, he knew what awaited him if he lost Celise as well.

A heart broken once was difficult to handle.

A heart broken twice would be impossible to handle. A third bound one would never be able to bring him out of the agony he'd fall into.

"Please, Celise. Promise me," he begged as he kept moving inside her. He couldn't stop. The bond demanded closure. It screamed inside him, pushed him on.

It fogged his mind, and before Wind knew it, he was lost in a world of pleasure. He thrust hard and fast, his passion taking them higher as her whimpers mixed with his groans, and he wasn't able to hold back anymore.

He lifted his upper-body and cried out. His body shook, his muscles shuddered as he filled her with his release. Ecstasy was mind blowing, and the heat in his eyes returned; intensifying his orgasm as his eyes flashed for the third and final time.

He was bound the Celise now, and his bond to Diane was forever sealed away.

Warm and exhausted, he collapsed on top of his new bound one, his new heart. His breathing came hard, but slowly, he returned to himself.

Celise smiled at him as she grabbed his face between her hands. "I promise."

The love he felt for her filled every part of his body when he heard her words.

It was strong, stronger than anything he'd ever felt for Diane.

And it was there to stay.

CHAPTER 28

Blaze's medical room was filled with a deafening silence. The air felt thick, and everyone seemed to be waiting for a bomb to go off.

The two Fighters, Nightmare, and Blaze, leaned against the wall near the double doors with tense expressions.

Their gazes were set on Wind, and Celise didn't blame them. If any of them dared to come any closer, he'd attack. He'd do anything to defend her.

He sat behind her on the bed with an arm around her.

Faye sat on one of the beds, watching with anticipation.

"So ... what have *you* been doing these past four hours?" Celise asked to ease the tension.

Faye lit up. "I've spend some time with the Fighters we saw in the gathering room."

Celise winced, surprise washing over her. "You did? What was that like?"

"I must admit, I expected the worst at first, but it turns out they are a bunch of teddy bears."

Nightmare frowned. "Teddy bears?"

"Well, you left me there and walked away, so don't tell me they weren't when you didn't see. They were unsure at first, but once I showed them how to relax, they couldn't get enough of me." Her eyes sparkled. "Every single one wanted me to sit on their lap or hug me. They even fed me, and couldn't stop talking. It was really sweet."

The leader put his palm to his forehead and sighed. "Unbelievable."

Blaze only chuckled.

Celise's jaw dropped as she stared at her. "You initiated a bond with Silver. Nightmare told them you're his bound one, so they figured they could touch you. They knew they wouldn't become bound to you."

Faye scratched her head and wrinkled her nose. "Well, yeah ... I kind of figured that one out when one of them asked if I'd sleep with him. He told me his bond screams desperately for a woman, and that he misses sex, but he refuses to bind himself again."

Blaze only laughed louder.

"I hope you didn't agree," Celise said, almost unable to hold back a giggle herself.

Wind seemed to be relaxing as well. He chuckled beside her.

Faye looked taken aback. "Of course not! Who do you take me for?"

She shrugged. "Just asking."

Nightmare moved away from the wall, frustration lingered in his shining eyes. "Can we talk about what matters now?" The cheerful mood in the room was put to death. He turned his gaze to Wind and Celise. "I guess the bonding went well?"

"Yes," Celise said. Heat traveled to her cheeks when Faye grinned. They all knew what she and Wind had done these past few hours.

He was bound to her now.

Her greatest dream had come true.

"I assume you know what happened to me," Wind said with a cold voice.

"What do you *think* happened to you?" Nightmare asked.

Her cyborg went silent for a while. "When I saw Diane was dead, my bond to her instantly went crazy. I assumed I was going to die. I've never felt a pain like that. I panicked and fled, but sometime during my escape, the bond started to behave differently. I expected it to just stop functioning and kill me, but it was just as strong as always." Wind took a deep breath, his arms tightened around Celise's waist. "Seconds before I lost consciousness, I realized the bond is only a disguise."

Faye winced. "What are you talking about?"

"The bond is a hidden poison, programmed to be released into a cyborg's system the moment the bound one dies. Up until then, the bond makes sure we stay with our bound one through love."

She flew up on her feet. "What? Are you serious?"

Wind sighed. "The bond was always real to me. I believed the Fighters who thought the bond was a lie, were crazy, but now, when I experienced the truth myself, I know better."

"I can't believe it." Anger lingered in Faye's voice. "Shade never mentioned any poison."

"That's because I tried to replace the bond with another signal. His bond had no reason to transform into the poison since his bound one was still alive," Nightmare said.

Faye frowned. "Shade said the reason you Fighters survive is because a small part of the bond remains inside you."

"It does, but only because it failed to kill us, but as you see on Wind, my signal blocks it successfully. Only the need for a bound one remains, and don't worry. I've scratched the plan I used on Shade."

Celise didn't say anything. She sat still in Wind's arms, sorrow filling her heart. Hearing Wind say the bond was a poison was like throwing a huge rock straight in her face.

Everything she knew, everything she'd learned was fake.

MedAct had lost her trust.

Faye thumped down on the bed again, disbelief in her eyes. "I can't believe it."

"I can examine you," Blaze told Wind, "but I guess it's not necessary. Your old bond is locked away, isn't it?"

He nodded. "Yes, I can't even sense it anymore. My new bond to Celise has completely taken over."

"How about your feelings for your first bound one?" Nightmare asked. "Are they still there?"

Celise tensed.

"Strangely enough, they are," Wind said. "I expected them to disappear, but at the same time, Jade *did* tell us my feelings for Diane would remain."

Nightmare nodded to himself, as if to confirm what Wind had said. "That's because the feelings are the only thing that *is* real. The bond forces them upon us, but once they are there, they become real. The bond was never designed to delete the emotions. Why should it, when you were supposed to die anyway?"

Celise breathed a sigh of relief and was able to smile.

Wind's arms tightened around her again, and he kissed her cheek. Maybe he understood what she was thinking, and wanted to comfort her. *Her* emotions were, without a doubt, real.

245

She'd always loved him, and always would.

"You all still love your late bound ones?" she asked.

Blaze nodded. "One way or another, yes, and trust me, it's not easy to live with, especially when our bonds scream inside us to find a new bound one. Some of us terminate themselves because it becomes too much."

"Sure, we could find a new bound one, and get peace of mind, but human life is so fragile," Nightmare said, "and I refuse to allow a woman have such power over me ever again." His voice was cold and harsh.

Celise looked at her hands. Yesterday, this conversation would've been surreal. Being in this place was surreal enough, but today, she believed every single word.

Before Nightmare, Faye, and Blaze had come back, she'd examined Wind using the cyborg medic's equipment, and the truth had been thrown in her face. Everything Wind said was true.

She no longer saw any reason to distrust Blaze and Nightmare.

Celise wanted to know more. She wanted to know everything.

Whatever MedAct was up to, she'd find out.

She couldn't trust Jade anymore. She was the head of MedAct, after all. She probably knew all of this.

Celise met Nightmare's dark glare. "I assume you don't know how to remove the bond yet."

"I thought I did when I tried it on Shade. I never believed it would almost kill him."

"Tell me about it."

The leader studied her. Then he smiled. "You believe us."

Celise took a deep breath. "Yes. I saw the facts in Wind's programming before you all came back. They speak a clear language."

Nightmare grinned. "Good."

Anticipation shone in Blaze's eyes. "I look forward to working with you, Celise."

She gave him a smile. "Me too."

Nightmare seemed to have gained new energy. "Tell me, Celise. Have you heard of Alexander Fleming?"

She frowned but nodded. "Of course. He was the CEO of MedAct before Jade Silva. He walked out of his office one day about fifteen years ago, and was never seen again."

"Exactly." The leader went to his desk. He looked through a drawer and pulled something out before approaching her.

Wind hauled her closer but didn't say anything.

"Here," Nightmare said and handed her a small portable hard disk. "Take it. I have plenty more. Everything you need to know is stored there."

"Like what?" Faye asked.

He sat down. "Alexander Fleming and I weren't friends,

247

but we spoke a few times. He took over Carolyn William's work after she'd died. He was just a kid when it happened, but for some reason, she left everything to him in her will. How he was related to her, I don't know. As an adult, he took over MedAct." Nightmare took a deep breath. "Alexander never expected to find what he found."

"What?" Celise asked.

Nightmare nodded toward the small disk. "He discovered that the bond is fake. Just like everybody else, he'd been told cyborgs can't exist without the bond, but when he saw that wasn't true; he started working in the dark. He didn't trust the members of the board who ran MedAct with him. He created an algorithm that's supposed to eliminate the bond for good, without damaging the cyborg, but he disappeared before he was able to finish it. He gave it to me, and I've been trying to finish it ever since." He sighed. "I was sure I had it right when I tested it on Shade, but I chose to ignore an important detail Alexander told me." He met Celise's gaze. "Take a look at it. You're one of MedAct's students, after all."

She swallowed and flipped the disk in her hands. It felt like she was holding the world's most cherished treasure. "I will."

He smiled. Determination shone in his eyes, and for the first time since she'd met him, she saw hope.

"Do you know why there aren't any female cyborgs?"

Blaze asked.

Celise winced, hadn't expected the question. "What I learned was that the female cyborgs required another type of programming, and Carolyn just wasn't able to make it work." She watched Blaze and Nightmare, who studied her in return. Then she sighed. "I guess that's a lie, too?"

The medic nodded. "We don't know if there has ever been any female cyborgs, but what we do know is that Alexander discovered a connection between the bond and the female cyborg programming."

Her heart stuttered. "What kind of connection?"

"We have no idea."

"That's what I chose to ignore when I tested my signal on Shade. We just couldn't find it, and thought Alexander could've been wrong," Nightmare said.

She blinked, stunned by the news. "The program for a female cyborg, is it in here as well?" She raised the disk with shaky hands.

He nodded. "Yes."

Silence filled the room for what felt like an eternity.

"Have you tried—?" Wind finally asked.

"No," Blaze answered. "We don't have the equipment to create a cyborg, but believe me, if we did, I'd be working on it right now. If the answer to saving all cyborgs from the bond lies in the female cyborg programming, then I want to be the one who discovers it."

Celise took a deep breath, overwhelmed by everything that had happened this day. "How much does Jade know?"

"We suspect she knows enough," Blaze answered.

She stood. "I guess that means we have a lot to do. Take me to them."

Nightmare frowned. "Take you to who?"

"The Fighters. I want to meet them."

CHAPTER 29

Celise held Wind's hand as the five of them walked down the hallways leading toward the big gathering room they'd passed to reach Blaze's medical room.

Celise had never imagined she'd find herself in this situation, but what was important was that Wind had survived.

Her examination had shown that he was all right. There weren't any traces left of the poison that'd been meant to kill him. She was grateful for that.

As they approached the gathering room, her nerves rose. She really didn't like being in the center of attention, but today, she had no other choice. If she was ever going to understand what was going on, she had to be able to communicate with the Fighters.

Celise had heard so many different stories about them over the years, mostly how dangerous and untrustworthy they were, but after listening to Faye's experiences, her thoughts had started to change. But one thing she did know for sure. The Fighters *were* damaged, one way or another. The poison had probably gotten the chance to spread long enough in some of them to create severe damage.

Silence filled the vast room as they entered, and at least twenty pairs of eyes turned toward them.

"Hello, boys!" Faye called out to the Fighters. "Have you missed me?"

They answered with smiles and grins, but no one spoke. Their focus was on Celise.

She glanced around. This time, she got a better look at the Fighters. Last time, she'd been under pressure to save Wind. She was under pressure this time as well, but it was different now. These Fighters knew she was a doctor working for MedAct, and MedAct wasn't a positive thing in their vocabulary.

Tension shot high inside her. Hopefully, none of the Fighters would try to hurt her.

She moved closer slowly, with Wind glued to her side. Her tension was mirrored in him.

The Fighters were spread out all over the room. Some sat, others stood. Their advent had interrupted gameplay, and the TV was on.

She couldn't tell what was wrong with these Fighters, or

if there even was anything wrong with them. But judging by their tired eyes, they all seemed worn out. Their bonds probably screamed on daily bases inside them to go after a new bound one.

From the corner of her eye, Celise noticed a Fighter sitting by a table. He hadn't looked up when they'd entered the room. Instead, he leaned over it with his hands under his head. His body shook. A book lay open in front of him. Maybe he'd tried to read, but the pain he seemed to be in, had probably made it impossible.

Instinct pulled at her, and she approached the Fighter.

Wind followed, and so did everybody else. A crowd gathered around her with Blaze, Faye, and Nightmare in the front.

Her cyborg placed himself just next to her, just in case the Fighter tried anything.

"How many of you are there?" Celise asked Nightmare.

"Around fifty."

"I only see about twenty in here. Where are the others?"

"Locked up."

Celise froze and shot her gaze to the leader's. "Why?"

"Because they are too damaged."

She scanned the room for a specific face, but he wasn't there. "Silver?"

"He's one of them," Nightmare said. "The need to bond with Faye is taking over. If I hadn't locked him up, he'd be running around up there, trying to find her."

Faye crossed her arms over her chest and snorted, turning her back to Nightmare.

Celise focused on the Fighter at the table. There was nothing she could do for Silver right now. The only one who could help him was Faye, and she didn't seem interested.

"Hello?" she said to the Fighter. "My name is Celise, but you probably know who I am, don't you?"

He nodded as he looked up.

She was taken aback when she looked into his shiny eyes. She'd never seen such big eyes before. They were mesmerizing, and they made her feel like he stared right into her soul, but there was also so much discomfort and exhaustion written all over his face.

Something told her he wouldn't last much longer. He'd probably been in this state since he'd lost his bound one. The poison must've made quite a number on him.

"Nightmare told us who you are," the Fighter said with a low voice.

Celise swallowed and shifted her weight to her other leg. "Is it all right if I examine you?"

A gasp went through the room, and tension rose.

The Fighter's gaze landed on Blaze.

"Let her," the medic told him. "She knows more about cyborgs than I do. It's her specialty."

"Very well." He looked at her. "Go ahead, but I don't know what you can do for me. My time is coming to an end."

She placed her bag on the table and pulled out her scanner as the Fighter took off his shirt. She glimpsed at Wind, almost expecting him to protest, considering what'd happened when she'd examined Shade, but her cyborg didn't move.

Instead, he gave her a nod.

Celise took a deep breath and pushed a few buttons. "What's your name?"

"Sense."

She smiled at him. "Nice to meet you, Sense."

He didn't answer, but he gave her a weak smile.

"Have you examined him?" she asked Blaze.

"Yes, but my knowledge of the cyborg anatomy is limited. I noticed it's similar to a human's, but there are differences, too. Unfortunately, not many Fighters let me take a better look at them, so I stand mostly without answers."

Celise watched the scan. A silent minute passed by. She tried to ignore all the eyes on her, but focusing on Sense alone wasn't easy. Her hands shook, and her breathing was ragged. Finally, the device finished, and it was as she'd thought. She turned to Sense, looking into his beautiful eyes.

Compared to many other of the Fighters, he seemed rather thin. Maybe he hadn't been able to eat well because of the pain. His dark brown hair needed a brush, and he also seemed to need some sleep.

"The poison from your bond has affected your nervous system. I assumed it took a while before Nightmare could help you?"

Sense nodded slowly. "The bond wasn't able to kill me, but it caused severe damage. I can barely walk without hurting all over. At my worst days, it spreads to my head, causing huge migraines. Last time, it took two weeks for me to recover from the attack."

Celise licked her lips. "I can help you, but you must be willing to go through it."

Interest awakened in his eyes. "Anything."

She nodded and dug out an electric needleless syringe, along with a bottle filled with transparent liquid. She placed the syringe on the glass bottle, and it filled without her needing to open it. The advantage with these syringes was that everything remained sterile, and she could use it even if she hadn't washed her hands. "This is a painkiller for cyborgs. Humans can't use it. It has no effect on us since our bodies function a little bit differently. If I inject you with this, the pain will go away, but you'll need a new dose every week."

Relief and hope filled his eyes. "Do it."

Celise hesitated. "There's a catch."

"What catch?" His face tensed again.

"For it to work, I have to inject it directly into your nervous system, and that'll hurt if you're conscious."

"Oh." Sense didn't seem so sure anymore.

"You'll only be out for a few minutes, and when you wake, the pain will be gone."

He went quiet, and all she could do was wait.

None of the other Fighters moved, but when she looked around, many seemed intrigued. She met the gazes of some of them, and they watched with anticipation. Even Wind and Faye seemed interested, but she had a hard time reading Nightmare. He looked angry, but also as if he wanted to know more.

Sense finally sighed. "Fine. Shall I go to the infirmary?"

"No, that's not necessary. Just sit here, and relax." Celise placed herself behind the Fighter and grabbed his neck.

He tensed under her touch.

She knew this move inside out. All doctors at MedAct trained it over and over again until it sat in the bone marrow. "This won't hurt," she assured as she pressed her hand against his spine, then her thumb and pinky simultaneously felt for the right places. When she found them, she pressed a little bit harder.

Sense's body went instantly slack, and he exhaled.

Celise slowly rested his head and arms on the table.

Shock seemed to go through every cyborg in the room. They stared at her with wide eyes and dropped jaws.

Blaze approached her. "How did you do that?"

She blinked and tensed when some of the Fighters took a step back. Had she done the right thing? "Cyborgs have a nerve in their necks that humans don't. MedAct made us study it over and over again until we knew exactly how to affect it. With the right touch, we can take you out for a few minutes." She met the medic's gaze. "It's your weak point."

"Fuck," Nightmare mumbled. The rage in his eyes was unmistakable. "I guess you have a lot to teach us, Celise."

She frowned. "I thought you knew about this."

He shook his head. "No, I've never seen it in use. Besides, until Blaze came along, I never had a medic on my team."

Celise only nodded, but worry followed. "This bottle is all I have. It'll last for tree more injections, but then I'll be out, and I won't be able to help Sense anymore. Jade will become suspicious if I start asking for meds too often." She winced as the room filled with grinning Fighters.

"Don't worry," Blaze said. "We'll make sure you have the supplies you'll need. I already have plenty in the medical room, but if there's something else, just let me know, and some of us will get it for you."

She frowned, didn't really like the sound of that. "How exactly?"

"Well—"

"I changed my mind. I don't want to know."

Blaze only chuckled. "As you wish, but I think you already know what I was about to say."

"Yeah, I probably do." Celise raised the syringe toward Sense's neck. She felt for the right place with her other hand, and when she found it, she gently injected the liquid.

The Fighters' gazes were fixed on Sense, waiting for him to wake up.

This was probably the most exciting thing they'd experienced in ages.

After a few minutes, Sense groaned as he lifted his head from the table.

Everyone in the room took a step closer.

Sense rubbed his neck and frowned. "My neck feels numb."

"That's just a side effect. It'll pass in a few minutes. How do you feel otherwise?"

The expectation in the room rose as the Fighter tested his body. He stood, and she moved back, surprised by how tall he was.

He stretched his limbs and rolled his head before he met her gaze and grinned. "The pain is almost gone. I can still feel it deep down, but the edge of it is gone."

Celise smiled. "Give it a few hours. Before nightfall, you should be pain-free."

His grin softened as gratitude filled his eyes. "Thank you, Celise. You've given me my life back. My bond still screams for a new bound one, but I can live with that now that the hurting is gone."

Joy filled her, and a feeling of satisfaction followed. Helping cyborgs was what she lived for, it was her passion, and she'd just saved a cyborg who'd likely put a bullet through his head in the near future if she hadn't.

Cheers broke out in the room, making her jump. Fighters applauded and yelled praise.

Heat traveled to her cheeks, and she grasped for Wind.

He grabbed her hand and pulled her to him. She didn't miss the pinch of pride she saw there.

Even Faye seemed thrilled.

Their fate had caught up with them, and it was time to change it.

CHAPTER 30

"Are you sure about this?" Celise asked Faye.

They stood in the forest next to her car. Nightmare and Blaze had driven them back to the place they'd first met.

Faye nodded, but insecurity was in her eyes. "I'm sure. I'm staying. I have to deal with Silver somehow. Just don't forget to stop by my house and pick up a few things for me."

She nodded. "We'll be back in a few days after we've buried Diane. I also have a few appointments with some cyborgs. I have to make sure Jade doesn't suspect anything. She's supervising Wind and me."

Nightmare handed her a cell phone. "Here, take this. Use it if you need to get in contact with us, but keep it hidden."

Celise nodded again, smiling at him. She'd never expected to see him in a new light. He still reminded her of that dangerous, unpredictable, and stern Fighter she'd seen many times on the news, but now, she also saw a gentler side to him. It was a side he probably didn't show often, but something told her he'd chosen to trust her now.

"Thank you," she said. "I will."

Wind crossed his arms over his chest. "Shade and Phoebe aren't going to like this."

Nightmare's gaze shot to him. "You intend to tell him?"

"Of course. Considering what you did to him, even if your intentions were good, he has the right to know. They both do. Besides, we can prove to him what's going on now. He'll be pissed, but he'll accept it eventually."

The leader's jaw tensed, and anger lit his eyes.

"I don't care if you like it or not," Wind said. "You wanted to hurt me too, to find answers, so even if I now know what you say is *true*, don't assume you and I will be friends. Besides, if you want to free all cyborgs from the bond, you're going to need as much support as possible."

Wind and Nightmare glared at each other, flinging invisible arrows.

"Wind's right," Faye said, turning to Nightmare. "You're going to need all the help you can get."

His gaze only darkened. "What if they talk?"

"Don't worry," Celise said, trying to calm him. "We'll make sure they won't. I know Phoebe and Shade well."

Nightmare didn't seem pleased. "Fine."

They said goodbye and got in the car. Celise waved to the Fighters and Faye as they drove away. She hoped her friend would be all right. Who knew what awaited her alone with these cyborgs, and especially with Silver. Celise couldn't help but worry. Nightmare had said Silver was locked up. Where, she didn't know, but probably somewhere deep within their underground compound.

And something told her Silver was angry ... *very* angry.

It was silent inside the car for several minutes as Wind drove back to his and Diane's home.

Celise remembered her promise that they could live there once Diane was gone, and that day was now upon them. She hoped Wind still wanted that. It was his home, after all, his life, but maybe too many memories lived there. Maybe he wouldn't be able to get past that.

The sadness around them grew as they approached the beautiful home. Celise inhaled when the house came into view, tensing. She watched his face.

Wind seemed relaxed and focused on driving, but he wasn't able to hide the sorrow in his eyes.

When he noticed she was watching him, he spared her a glance.

To her surprise, he smiled.

Her cyborg placed his hand on her leg, as if to comfort her. "I know what you're thinking." He paused. "I still love her. My feelings are still there, but now, I also feel an inner calmness. She has finally found peace. It's over, and I don't have to worry about her anymore. She doesn't have to suffer anymore, and even if I miss her, I have to try to look at the future positively." Wind dried away a tear and gave her another smile. "I have you now, and I intend to make the best out of it. I love you, Celise. Don't ever doubt it. Even if the bond forced those feelings upon me, they *are* real, and they won't change. I want to make you happy."

His words warmed her heart. "I want to make you happy, too."

"Then let's make each other happy."

She smiled and nodded.

He parked in the driveway. They got out of the car and looked up at the house as they held each other's hands.

"Do you still want to live here?" Wind asked.

Celise held her breath. "Of course. Do you?"

He gently squeezed her hand. The gratitude shone in his eyes. "Yes, I wish to stay. My past is here, but I want my future to be here as well ... with you. Thank you."

Their future didn't seem easy now that they were involved with the Fighters, but they'd always have each other.

They kept staring at the house. They couldn't avoid what they had to do next. It filled Celise's heart with an unavoidable ache.

Eventually, Wind started walking, never releasing her

hand, and she followed. He opened the front door.

It was almost too quiet, and even the sounds of her own breaths sounded too loud.

Everything was as they'd left it, with the bright staircase in front of them, and the chandeliers in the ceiling still lit.

Her cyborg's grip on her hand tightened, and then he led her up the stairs, going to the guest room where Diane still lay. His breathing increased with each step they took, and when they finally stood in the doorway, he was almost hyperventilating.

Celise had her bag—in case she had to try to save him again—but she couldn't save him from a broken heart.

Wind inhaled when he saw Diane's body lying where they'd left her. Her eyes were closed, but she looked peaceful. He sobbed and wiped away tears.

Celise let go of his hand when he moved toward his first bound one's body.

This was his moment. Wind needed this.

He needed time to grief, even if he'd said he'd tried to be happy.

Wind lifted Diane into his arms and placed her on the bed. He sat on the edge, caressing her cheek. His chin trembled, and he was unable to keep his hand steady.

There was so much love in that single caress.

Emotions wreaked havoc in Celise's heart, making her cry and ache as she watched the man she loved. She slowly approached Wind but didn't touch him. Something told her he didn't want to be touched right now.

Celise could almost feel his pain, and she wished she could say or do something to ease his agony, but there was nothing no one could do.

He laid his head against Diane's chest and wept.

CHAPTER 31

"Thank you for the medicine, Celise. I really appreciate it. My stomach already feels better."

She smiled at the brown-haired cyborg. He was at least a head taller than her and built like a dancer. It wouldn't surprise her if he was one, but she wasn't familiar with either him, or his bound one, who stood next to him with a wide smile by the front door. "You're welcome, Trance," Celise said. "Make sure to take one pill every day to calm your stomach fluids, and stay away from the candy. You might be a cyborg, but too much candy isn't good for anyone."

He blushed. "It was so good, and I've never tasted candy before, but I've learned my lesson. I should've listened to Abby when she told me not to eat too much." He gently squeezed his woman's hand.

"We just left MedAct a few days ago," Abby told Celise.

"Everything is still new to him." There was so much love and happiness in her blue eyes.

She was a sweet-looking woman with blonde hair, and Celise could do nothing but wish them the best, but her new knowledge about the bond lingered in the back of her mind. "Congratulations," Celise said with a smile she didn't feel on the inside. "I hope your time together will be amazing."

"Thank you," Abby said, beaming with joy. "Are you a bound one, too?"

"Yes, Wind and I live here. He's upstairs right now, not wanting to disturb us."

They looked around with wide eyes, admiring the chandeliers and paintings.

"This is an amazing house," Trance said. "You've really created something beautiful together. Was your time at MedAct with Wind just as eventful as mine was with Abby? I haven't gotten the chance to talk to another cyborg about it yet."

She hesitated. "I never spent time with Wind at MedAct when he was newborn. I'm his second bound one."

That wiped the grins off their faces, and she regretted telling them.

"I'm sorry to hear that," Abby said. "Is he ... all right?"

She nodded, giving them another smile to ease the sudden pressure filling the hallway. "He's still a little bit sad, but we're getting there."

"That's good. Let us know if you'd like to spend some time with us. That might take his mind off of things."

Celise liked this couple more and more. "I appreciate it."

They both gave her a hug before they left.

She closed the door behind them, breathing in air deeply into her lungs. This was the first time she'd received a patient at home, but she liked it. Usually, she went to her patients' homes. Besides, she didn't want to leave Wind, and taking him with her could've created an unnecessary scene.

He still felt overwhelmingly overprotective of her, but he was able to stay in another room. He'd told her how difficult it'd been to watch her take care of Sense, but the Fighter had needed help, and he'd pushed his instincts aside the best he could.

Celise headed upstairs.

Wind was in his study painting, and she looked forward to seeing what he was creating.

Since they'd buried Diane two days ago, he'd spent almost every waking minute in there. Whenever he needed a break, he came running to her, but he wouldn't let her see his painting. He wanted her by his side as much as possible, and Celise didn't mind it at all.

She opened the door, and the scent of fresh paint hit

her. It made her lips twitch. She spotted Wind on the other side of the room, standing in front of a canvas with his back toward the huge windows.

It was bright outside, and he seemed to be in a good mood. Fresh paint spots decorated his loose pants and bare chest as he worked on his masterpiece. In her eyes, he was a masterpiece himself.

His rippled muscles and big biceps made her mouth water as arousal spread through her, settling between her legs. She couldn't wait to wash the paint off of him like she'd done last night.

Celise slowly approached but didn't move in front of the canvas. She wouldn't until he wanted her to see the painting.

Wind's eyes lit up when he spotted her. "Did everything go well?"

"Yes. Trance still has a lot to learn, but he seems eager to do it, and his bound one is walking on clouds."

He chuckled. "Yes, I remember that time. It was both amazing and confusing."

Wind had spent hours crying next to Diane's body after they'd gotten home.

Celise had just sat next to him, giving him her support, but once the tears had dried, they'd been gone for good.

They'd called the funeral home, who'd come a few hours later, and taken her body to prepare for the funeral.

He'd made love to Celise that night with pure passion and longing. Wind had never held onto her the way he'd done that night. Afterward, they'd fallen asleep in each other arms.

"How's the painting coming?" she asked, trying to focus on his face, but his appealing body made her gaze rake over him with hunger in her gut.

He raised an eyebrow when he noticed. "I'm almost done, but you seem more interest in other things."

Heat seared her face. "Well, I can't help it when you're dressed like that. You're too tempting."

Wind laughed and put the brush on the table next to the canvas. The surface was filled with all kinds of different containers of paint and dirty water. He gave her a wicked grin and pulled down the top of his pants, revealing a part of his hip bone, but hiding all the other deliciousness he had there.

Celise winced as her sex clenched with need. "Now you're just mean."

He pulled her into his arms, but moved her around, with her back to his chest as he chuckled. "I love teasing you, and I'll tease you more in just a little while, but first, what do you think of the painting?"

Celise turned her gaze to the canvas and gasped. He'd created a beautiful sunset in delicate and colorful colors, and in the sky, she saw him, herself, and Diane holding each other with closed eyes and peaceful smiles. "Oh, wow. It's amazing."

His arms tightened around her. "This is my way of saying goodbye to the past. I'll cherish it always in my heart, and I'll remember it with a smile. It was a wonderful time, but life moves on, and now I'm here, with you, and I'll stay with you, no matter what happens. Bond, or no bond." He pressed his lips above her ear. "I'll always love you, Celise." His voice was like a seductive whisper, filled with exciting promises.

She turned to him with a lump in her throat, caressing his face, and looking deep in his eyes.

Wind was the man she loved.

She'd loved him ever since she'd laid eyes on him. She'd suffered in silence ever since, but now, they were here ... *together*. It'd been a long and tough journey, but they had their whole lives in front of them to make the best out of it.

Celise gently kissed him. "I love you, too."

"I love hearing you say that."

"Then I'll make sure to say it as often as you need to hear it, but first ..." She looked down. Despite the loose pants, he wasn't able to hide the bulge he sported. "I intend to take care of you ... right here, right now."

His body jerked when she slipped her hand inside his pants and grabbed his warm hard cock. His breathing came out ragged, but his grin widened. "Show me."

"Count on it."

She pressed her lips to his as she slowly began stroking him, showing him the passion she felt on the inside.

He answered with a groan.

From the corner of her eye, Celise noticed it became brighter in the room, and rays of light touched Wind's painting like a delicate caress. It gave her the feeling Diane was whispering her final goodbye, but it was also as if she was saying, '*He's yours now. Take good care of him for me*'.

And Celise promised she would.

THANK YOU

Thank you for reading my story! I hope you enjoyed it. Feel free to leave a review. I would love to hear your opinion. The third book in the series, *Kissed Cyborg*, Faye's and Silver's story, is next.

OTHER BOOKS BY NELLIE C. LIND

THE ELDERS OF THE SEASONS SERIES:
Winter's Bride - Book 1 (2015)
Autumn's Lady - Book 2 (Coming soon)

BOUND BY HER SERIES:
Her Cyborg - Book 1 (2016)
Tempted Cyborg - Novella (2016) (Available through
mailing list)
Loved Cyborg - Book 2 (2017)
Kissed Cyborg - Book 3 (coming soon)

ENCHANTED EVER AFTER SERIES:
The Sacrifice - Book 1 (2014) (Available for free)
The Monster Under the Bed - Book 2 (2014)
Within a Heartbeat - Book 3 (2015)
Deny Me If You Can – book 4 (2014)

THE BLOOD OF ANGELS SERIES:
Angel in Chains - Book 1 (2014)